CW01659224

HOW TO LOITER IN A TURF WAR

A NOVEL BY

COCO SOLID

PENGUIN BOOKS

PENGUIN

UK | USA | Canada | Ireland | Australia
India | New Zealand | South Africa | China

Penguin is an imprint of the Penguin Random House group of companies, whose addresses can be found at global.penguinrandomhouse.com.

Penguin
Random House
New Zealand

First published by Penguin Random House New Zealand, 2022

10 9 8 7 6 5 4 3 2 1

Design by Carla Sy © Penguin Random House New Zealand
Illustrations by Jessica Hansell
Cover illustration by Jessica Hansell
Author photograph by Todd Karehana and Julie Zhu
Prepress by Image Centre Group
Printed and bound in Australia by Griffin Press, an Accredited ISO AS/NZS 14001 Environmental Management Systems Printer

Thanks to the Pacific Arts team at Creative New Zealand and the Fulbright New Zealand whānau for their support.

A catalogue record for this book is available from the National Library of New Zealand.

ISBN 978-0-14-377858-5
eISBN 978-0-14-377864-6
ISBN 978-0-14-377982-7 (audio)

penguin.co.nz

MIX
Paper from responsible sources
FSC www.fsc.org FSC™ C009448

For my late daughter Te Hoia.

I only wanted you to see your name
in print when you got older.

I have to finish some stuff here they
reckon, but we'll be together soon bub.

CONTENTS

One

TE HOIA VS. THE WAIT

It starts with the shopfronts
Then they cripple our slang
Someone calls the noise police
Party ends with a bang

Piopi Ruta-Chris, *Selected Writings 1989–2002*

TE HOIA KNOWS THE CONCRETE WALL has already started to boil under the sun. Her denim ass predictably caramelises as she leans against it anyway. She is inattentive and sick of using both knees.

She touches her earrings. Buses involve a lot of waiting. Squinting. Whenever she touches her jewellery it sounds like a cutlery drawer up close.

At least no one else can hear this jangle.

Or my busted lungs.

Or the random creaks of my body quite like I can.

Why the hell is it so hot today anyway?

Climate change better not fuck up my Matariki.

Te Hoia runs her fingers through the interlocking chains and charms on her wrist.

She remembers a disgusting analogy her friend Rosina once made up.

Riding New Zealand buses, same as riding dick.

You need to be optimistic your next one won't let you down despite what you know.

You let a bus timetable lie to your face.

But you still get on board don't you?

I'm just saying. If you and them are going the same way . . . why not hop on?

Te Hoia shudders and smiles; how the straights find the perseverance she'll never know.

She thinks of Rosina. She thinks of her friends.

Their cluster of mongrel islands. Messy with safety and joy.

Rosina is an aspiring art jerk. She's Hawaiian, Rarotongan, Sāmoan and . . .

Was it Irish?

I can't remember what her dad is.

I know he beefs with the Queen too.

Wait, yep. Irish. Pretty sure it was Irish.

Rosina is noisy. She reminds Te Hoia of . . .

Five different-sized pots tumbling out of a cupboard.

Q says Rosina exudes the freedom of children who can yell at their parents.

Rosina relishes conflict and the words 'what's that supposed to mean?' should be tattooed on her neck (among the others already there). Rosina pretends she's not going to drink tonight but she does, usually to great effect. She likes spilling the secrets of her slower-mouthed friends, friends like Te Hoia. Last Wednesday she impulsively lopped her long black mane into a platinum blonde (or maybe it's more of a mustard) pixie cut, which Te Hoia has been processing and admiring since.

Little shit, she always looks incredible.

That bone structure takes no prisoners.

Rosina is selling some paintings tonight in a yuk part of town that Te Hoia hates. The girls have to go. No flaking allowed.

Dammit. I wonder how Q is getting into town.

Q is a bedroom poet who will probably leave the exhibition early because she gets up at 4am to work at the (best) bakery before the motorway. Q is Tongan-Fijian 'with a dash of Indian and Solomon'. Her long hair is always swept to one side; this has been dubbed 'the ramen sweep'. She has a soft voice which is lucky, as Q's words always prove the most lethal when pushed. Q is short for her now-ancient nickname Qrispy. This was given to her when she started working at the bakery. But an American franchise bearing a similar name had, predictably, opened next door. Where she lives, the deep-fried multinationals were becoming predatory so in protest she'd curtly graduated to the name Q. She even wrote the term 'food desert' instead of 'dessert food' on the bakery blackboard. She changed it back when someone implied she was a bad speller.

Te Hoia and Q have been friends for a long time, but lately their glances and secrets have felt a little deeper. Te Hoia has a slippery crush on her friend, but she won't allow herself to think about it too much.

Te Hoia is at university, studying political sciences.

'With an interest in gentrification law and environmental racism.'

I've been rehearsing that.

She attributes this volatile interest to her two older brothers. Being terrified of her cuteness as a toddler, they decided to radicalise their sister from the age of three. Te Hoia is Māori and Filipina so finding her fire was never a problem. Her brothers just fast-tracked the process.

Te Hoia is now morbidly late for class (again) because of the bus (again). To catch it now is to favour spite over function. But the bus-stop knows how to make Te Hoia irrationally spiteful, so she waits.

A distant car-horn interrupts her blank stare.

Te Hoia knows a large bag at a desolate bus-stop is mandatory. From her underarm phone-booth she decides to pull out headphones and the bunch of chapped, stained essays. Her lovely lecturer Whetu printed them out for her the other day. She is an older Māori gay professor, so Te Hoia is learning how to be the teacher's pet for once.

The essays are all written by her favourite author, Piopi Ruta-Chris. She inspects the groovy photocopied books.

Look at this analogue shit. Paper.

Love this old font too.

I forget university was free once.

Everyone was having a blast, even the damn typographers.

While looking down at the papers, Te Hoia startles herself. She sees her outfit and realises she looks cuter than usual. A quick and welcome revelation.

See, why does no one drive past me when I look like this?

I look smart.

Why do people only cruise by when I'm bleeding through my skirt or have oily hair or have been crying about my broken brain?

Well, not today.

Gassed up, Te Hoia now stands swannish and posing with her papers. She enjoys her exterior success so much that for a few minutes she forgets she's actually meant to be reading. Her mind goes off on pinball tangents. Her focus starts to rattle harder than the road-works nearby. A lollipop man looks at her.

That's right. Behold the outfit bro—yes, she can dress.

Let me stand here till the bus comes.

Feel my tin earrings, hold my little book.

I'm gonna sway in whatever weather today throws at me, throw no tantrum about waiting.

'Stealth is wealth,' like my grandma's motto.

Te Hoia's nose crinkles for a moment. She's trying to celebrate looking sexy, not think about her deceased grandma.

God . . . what a weird motto.

Or should that be Gods . . . plural . . .

Whoever yous are, I know you're all eavesdropping on me!

She looks up, now paranoid. Her internal life and main character complex are wilding out.

I bet Māori and Filipino Gods eavesdrop more than other Gods too.

Why did I get that combo?

They stand around the fountain of youth like it's a watercooler.

Comparing notes with the Greek Gods about my psychotic thoughts.

Overheating, Te Hoia steps into a spindly shadow of the bus sign. She's more agitated by her imagination than impressed. Finally, she surrenders to the text in front of her.

Assorted essays by academic, lawyer and poet Piopi Ruta-Chris. Te Hoia chooses the first essay on the pile, 'Reupholstering Paradise: The Fever Dream of Fish Restaurants' taken from *Paradigms/Parody of Land Value in the South Pacific* © 1989.

This writer makes Te Hoia feel like everyone else, a rare feeling. Whenever she is sad she looks up old Piopi Ruta-Chris interviews schooling arrogant British dudes. VHS-scorched archival footage of a leading wāhine is a must when the racist news hurts your feelings. Piopi always wore a tiny flower in her hair and passed away too young, probably from doing the psychic labour of eighty white male professors. Piopi's work tethers Te Hoia to a knowing nod that she never thought she'd find inside an institution.

Te Hoia hasn't chosen her background music yet, but at least the headphones block out construction noises. She accepts the muffle is as good as it's going to get. She reads through her grimace.

> Settled land will always be appraised for a mutating sense of 'value'. This value requires selective memory and the decimation of all indigenous ideology in order to operate. Imperial scales and semantics will always move with the distrustful times in the South Pacific. But their agenda to erase and reupholster remains soldered to the stolen ground.
>
> Sanitised, colonised narratives often fixate on tangible, singular disputes — the invasion as an isolated moment, a clean cut of beef to serve in the history books. For who can neatly edit the intestinal syrups of countless murder scenes, the whispering and forgotten back-waters that wash against our collective memory while we sleep?

Te Hoia's dad said that this suburb was a thriving Māori settlement in the 1800s.

Before it did the whole . . . war colonial bloodbath thing.

She wonders if her bus-stop was once where a violent, historical moment had taken place.

These villas are all 'mutating in value'.

I guess people have always made a killing round here. One way or another.

Oceania is now navigating a new bulldozing model. With gentrification, or 'urbanization initiatives', we can now experience multiple upheavals and cosmetic transformations within one suburb, not just one city. Be it Suva, Honolulu, Auckland or Apia, we are now witnessing the hard-won 'city' being broken into an array of homogenised host-bodies. The stage is set for 'Death of a Salesman' but trust the impact of these letting agents shall live long after we are gone. Residential rupturing and fiscal satire — so much has happened since our people were pulled into the allure of early 'trade'.

Tonight I am hungry and I can almost smell the whipping fish nets of old. Be they earnest backpacker or depraved pilgrim, it is seldom a grand ambition that lures a supposed saviour to stay. History quietly dictates it is often a private and banal detail that satiates the colonial assertion that they rightfully belong.

Our needs in the modern age may seem more esoteric, complicated. But they aren't. The reconnaissance and beloved chicanery of our new-wave bounty hunters are no less primal and specific. The racket is the same, it just has a more attractive typeface. Nice space you have here, sure would be a shame if something legislative were to happen to it.

We noble natives have long understood the sleek shifts of word play that are always moving underfoot. Revitalisation. 'This area has cleaned up a lot.'

Your neighbourhood is the new target. We are as vulnerable to confiscation today as we always were. Within every dealing and exchange we walk the plank. The can(n)on claps probably still ring in your ancestral ears. Your blood intuitively recalls the 'value' of your land even if you have no idea. Our right to identify and express all we are historically wrongfully bereft of eludes us, until the eviction notice helps us remember. Our friends leave. Our favourite people can't make rent.

And who is to say that the scent of fresh fish on a fire did not enhance the Crown's fever for what we thought we'd always have. Real estate agents put on pots of coffee before selling a house after all. And Māori cannot smell our own shorelines without the Crown's permission. This essay is now fish fan fiction, I am still hungry.

Some friends of mine moved into a neighbourhood just to be closer to the earthy smells of a legendary restaurant. We still speak of how good our last meal tasted before the restaurant's rent started to mysteriously levitate.

> I often wonder, is that meal the restaurant's true legacy? That spicy oily plate haunts me better than any Victorian child. Where do I go for a decent fish curry now?

Te Hoia's gut fauna assemble into an angry fist. The essays sag in her fingers. This was written in 1989 and yet today here she lurks, looking at the tomb of Salties (the closed fish 'n' chip shop from her childhood). Currently morphing into . . .

A dog groomer and . . . jeweller!?

A throttling drill noise nearby pops her in the ear. The sound of machinery is now deafening. A bad day at the bus-stop can sometimes feel like a symphony of bullshit.

I'll tell you where we can get our fish from Piopi.

Nowhere.

Te Hoia lifts her head.

All this internal uprising and yet no sign of the bus, only tiny trucks up ahead. She closes one eye and calculates: one faraway truck, if shrunk, could drive perfectly through her bracelet latch. These are the shameful activities she resorts to while waiting. The essay whispers for her to finish reading it.

OK, but gotta be quick.

Y'know. Just in case the bus comes.

Te Hoia gazes up the road one more time, holding the papers over her baked line of vision. Between the bus arriving late and the spluttering asphalt (which she now realises is just a remixed cannon clap) Te Hoia wonders which is going to break her spirit first.

TWO

THANK YOU DRIVER

A FEW MINUTES LATER (after Te Hoia has choreographed her grisly roadside death perfectly) the bus arrives. It lands at her feet with a hydraulic groan and shrug. Te Hoia scans her bus card.

Metal belly-laughs rumble below; onboard her fingers quickly suckle the beams — she's almost forgotten that she was mad. Almost. There are stylish terracotta swirls on the seats, for once the ugly designs don't give her vertigo. Te Hoia moves to swing herself into a seat but a soft voice throws itself down the aisle.

— Hoia.

A satin ball — she knows that voice. Te Hoia turns with what the girls jokingly call her 'resting intergenerational trauma face', her brow still annoyed from the hot wait outside. Sitting at the back is Q. The girls burst out laughing as they clock each other. It's the bumping-into equivalent of a decent Christmas present.

— Girl, come to the back!

Te Hoia stands and dashes to the back seat before the otherwise empty bus pulls out and knocks her off-balance. Q is wearing a woollen top that flaunts her lean frame. It's a deep-dyed maroon with random flecks of white.

— Sis that top reminds me of marbled meat at PAK'nSAVE.

In an extremely cute way.

Q beams.

— I'm a tightly wrapped steak.

— A high-protein snack.

In this life and maybe a couple of others, Te Hoia and Q have laughed a lot together.

Q is a tall design, angular. Rosina once described Q best.

Her bones are a breeze to draw when the pencils are sharp enough.

Te Hoia on the other hand is composed of succulent swerves and circles. Her feet can't touch the ground once she sits down on the bus-seat but, horizontally, she takes up two. She heavily identifies with the toffee waves being churned in the (constantly broken) ice-cream machine at Burger Queen. Yes, this city had a Burger Queen once. Unsurprisingly, it closed a week after Salties did.

Q snobbishly checks to see what Te Hoia is reading, but she already knows.

— Piopi. Again?

— Well, I would read your poems
if you'd hurry up and finish them.

— Girl, I work in a bakery.

— And?

— Yeah yeah. Rosina was hassling me too.

Q's shoulders cave in; she leans in to tell a juicy secret. She could read a shopping list like a love letter.

— Last night I had a dream. I went to a poetry reading . . .

— You lost me.

— . . . and the audience wanted to suck my bone marrow dry.
And not in a good way.
Like . . . zombies.

— So you don't like poetry readings.
No one does.

— I do though! I just don't like how all the Pālagi kids look at me when I go.

— You dream about them because
you need to overcome them.
You wanna be like them.

— I wanna get their scholarships.
That's about it.

— Put your book out!
Then just do what I do . . .
make them feel bad for what their
bloodlines did to yours.
Keep em on their toes.

— I don't want to.

— What? Why?
The guilt-trip is literally the only
perk we get.

— Maybe I might want to be . . . like . . . maybe I want to write some dumb bitch stuff about dogs! Ever think about that?

— Write about eating them,
more like.

— That's horse babe. If you're gonna be racist to Tongans at least get it right.

Te Hoia splutters a laugh. Q just smirks and tucks her hair behind her ear.

— Plus, who's gonna buy a bakery girl's poems?
Cos it won't be you!

Te Hoia waves her essays defiantly.

— Oi I read!

— Looks like photocopied Piopi
from the library.

— Yeah, well that's still ten cents a page.

— That your teacher paid for!

Te Hoia cackles from the laser-accurate wound.

— And look, my self-sabotage is too strong today. Even for the likes of you sis.
I have a loop in my head saying *stop stop stop*.
Pounding.
Like that Lotto shop that plays Bollywood all day.

Te Hoia knows the exact shop — and the feeling Q's describing.

— Plus, have you ever considered . . . if you have to fight nightly 'doing what you love', maybe you just don't love it that much?

Te Hoia isn't buying it, pursing her lips.

— Ah . . . am I making excuses now?

Te Hoia nods, but she gives a sympathetic hum under the engine racket. Anyone socially shat on and brainwashed knows that feeling. They watch a local Korean babe get on the bus. She has a honey bob and her parents run the $5 Mart (formally known as the $2 Mart). Sitting behind the driver, they watch her hair shimmy as they talk. Back and forth, with every corner. They're entranced by the silky car-wash.

— I'm just saying . . . I don't always have the muscle to fight that voice.
I feel like something is editing my thoughts and I gotta fight it every day. I'm tired.

— Fight?
Fight what?

— Fight all these demonic semantics for hours.

— Ooh, Demonic Semantics is
a good name for something.
What's your book called?

— *Releasings*. What ya think?

Te Hoia pauses then nods again; she likes it. It's very Q.

— See, anyone with a brain knows you're good Q.
Just self-publish a smash oi.
And we could stop taking the bus.

— You're the Māori. Get us some reparations.

— No babe.
A multi-island poet with humble bakery beginnings?
She's migrant! She's diaspora!
She sells herself.

— Take the Crown to the cleaners, for God's sake.
We could own this bus.

The bus driver looks at them in the jumbo mirror.

The girls realise they're yelling and pipe down.

They take a few moments to silently fantasise about their compensation-mobile. Q envisions a lot of powder blue and air-conditioning. Te Hoia hears an electric engine and anime jazz. Their bus would definitely have expensive speakers.

Someone's aunty hobbles onto the bus. Five big bags, a cute flowery dress under her polar-fleece (despite the heat) and a wiry silver bun.

Te Hoia trickles out of her thoughts.

— Well. Got anything I can read yet?

Q blinks.

— Just give me a break from rereading Piopi essays.
Please.
Show me.

The girls exchange a loaded stare.

Te Hoia's cheeks almost short-circuit looking at Q's features, but she fights it off.

Q is just thrilled someone gives a shit about her busted scripture.

She takes her phone out. After a few shy taps, Te Hoia takes the device from Q with a loving winch.

— 'Releasings. This is copyright, all rights reserved by Q.
Confidential, do not share.'

Ooh, it must be good then!

Getting smart to my uncle who thinks he's my dad

Wishful fathers unleash a lack
the air claps when they return.
Capillaries flood
our answers turn dumber.
We don't wanna seem 'up ourselves'.
Right Dad?
Be sure
to put a dad's power
into a jar
that only they can open.
Someone else's son appears.
A son with a lanyard.
A son who can't spell effeminate.
He asks to speak to the
head of the house.
My uncle puffs up the stairs.
My sister and I laugh until the lanyard leaves.
Oh fathers with their
roar acidic.
Father's father
legend has it he removed his own liver after
a blackout.
Father's father's father
he would probably say
Oh so you think you're smarter than me?

For once

The smarting hesitation
one feels
before they dip their mouth
into the verboten caramels
of their own slang.
I know you can't hear
dat lingual umami that
I'm spooning over
you and me.
That's because
the sizzle is silent.
But so many cycles ago
I learnt your way.
Why in this life
do you never learn mine?
Come in from the frost and
learn my way.
Burn Sugar.
Be a Sun,
just this once?

With a wave and shout to the driver, Te Hoia disembarks. She shakes her head at Q's terminally unreleased poetry and, now on the street, the two cross the hectic shopping centre car-park.

They walk in silence, apart from when they spot Ata, someone they went to school with. He's pushing an accordion of trolleys through the Hyundais. An excellent fade, a blasting smile, he is still covered in his same signature rosary and Jesus-centric jewellery he rocked in adolescence. Q mutters.

— Ugh. He is still annoyingly fine.

Te Hoia shrugs.

— I saw him working at the funeral home last month too.
Bro has multiple jobs. If you like that kinda thing.

Ata smiles, waving and, now aware of his attractive work ethic, Q waves back with her softest hand.

— I do like that kinda thing.
Maybe I should give him a poem as a hint.
That he won't get.
Because no one ever gets the hint when I do that.

— Tsss, you are such a poet.

They press on uncomfortably.

Three
IS THAT US?

THEIR STEPS SLOW. Up ahead they see a row of overheated girls in matching white t-shirts and loose buns atop their heads. They're dropping tubs of sliced onion onto a black plate and Q admires the wholesale canola oil sparkling in the sunlight. Te Hoia quickly recognises her distant cousin among those turning sausages on the grill. The two kiss each other's cheeks and immediately ask how the other and their mother has been. Q doesn't miss a beat, silently buying a sausage in bread while they talk. Te Hoia's cousin tells them it's a fundraiser for their nursing school.

— For an extra two dollars you get a free drink and a raffle ticket.
You go into the draw for a professional make-up artist session.

— True?

— Yeah. But it's just me and my old beauty school brushes.
Gotta multitask.
Girl, I know you know.

The two cousins crack up with an identical laugh, but the rogue raffle pitch is enough for Q to upgrade and buy a ticket. She plunges her wrist into the tub of icy cheap drinks and hands the girls another golden coin. Te Hoia wishes everyone luck. She and Q — hot dog in hand — step out onto the road again.

— You got a ticket?

— Yeah, I was thirsty.

And your cousin had decent
eyeliner skills, I can tell.

— Support the nurses and whatnot.
Oi can I have a bite?

Q hands the hot dog over. Te Hoia hums as the fluffy bread barely catches all the messy and juicy contents. Q sips on the technicolour something.

— Yo I love it when the meat and the butter and onion ratio is right.

— And these onions are
cooked good too.
Remember that one we got
that other time!?

— That school fundraiser, oh my gosh.
Where those kids gave us raw white onion!

— These sausages are real
good too.
I mean . . . they aren't boujee
but they're better than the
ones we have at the bakery.
So bad.

— Look at you Miss High Quality Meat connoisseur.

Muddling and joking as they go, the girls arrive at a cagey wasteland. They've unknowingly walked into a pop-up organic market. In the early twentieth century, this was where the Chinese gardeners and wedding dressmakers (who wisely refused to pay for a shop-front or flea-market stall) set up and made a surreptitious killing. The tradition remained until . . . well, now, it seems. The girls look around the tidy path, searching for some kind of familiarity. But all Asian presence has vapourised.

Q notices her crunchy budget wurst is being stared at by a prickly vendor, still waiting for 'real' customers to show up. Te Hoia and Q knew the neighbourhood was fast hurtling into this, but they're shocked it came so soon. The vendor has an apron covered in water-coloured prairie mice; her hair is waxy and frosted. At first the vendor's face is doughy and disarmingly sweet. She smacks her coral lipstick. But the girls feel uneasy, sensing she doesn't appreciate them stumbling into her cobble-stoned turf.

— It smells disgusting. And white bread is all sugar.

Conditioned, the girls politely smile. They want to check this white lady isn't joking.

— Meat is murder, you know.

Q looks bewildered at Te Hoia, tossing up between brutally enlightening this lady or a smile.

In contrast, Te Hoia's temper doesn't have the time to choose.

— So is colonisation, babe.

The other street vendors look around.

Q, seeing the vendor getting out her phone, quickly backs up Te Hoia with a snip.

— I admit, it's not gentrified cricket protein and I apologise, sis.

Q only uses sis when someone is a) like a sister, or b) not like a sister at all.

— Do you see this sign? No animal products.
You do the math — if you can.

Te Hoia's face caves in.

— 'If I can'?

Time slows down and ramps up simultaneously, like clashes of this kind tend to do. Voices start to shake. The lady gets her phone from her apron pocket. Te Hoia is too fast for her.

— I got a phone too. You wanna be famous today? Cos I can pay you in exposure, sis.

The vendor's face ripples back at them.

— I actually have every right to call the police right now.

The girls bahaha the tent down.

— Woah woah woah, what? Cos I ate a sausage on a public street? Sorry you literally have no right to call the cops.

Q whimpers 'bullshit' to (what she thought was) herself. The apron lady pounces.

— And I'm not going to put up with this kind of language either. I am allowed to run my business safely!

— Wow you heard me whisper a swear word?
And they say these streets aren't rough anymore!

People pause and start staring, a sheltered child even starts crying for dramatic effect.

Slowly, a ginger freckly uncle from another stall emerges, piping up. He looks like a spindly coat-rack with a white beard.

— These girls did nothing wrong, come on man. Leave it alone!

His tiny wife is rattled by the arguing; she anxiously moves their mānuka and rosemary soaps away from the bad vibes and vendor. The man's solidarity surprises the girls.

— You heard him, leave us alone!

— All I asked is that you get away from my stall while eating meat!

— Except that's not what you said is it!

Te Hoia is about to roll up her Piopi-essay-memorising sleeves, when they hear the islander *SSHHH*, followed by

— Oi!

It's Rosina. Her face is painted like a grey and green clown. She's guzzling some slime smoothie, rocking a maroon tracksuit and matching heels while motioning for them to hurry up. The jolting image of Rosina cognitively zaps them out of the confrontation. Te Hoia and Q look at each other. In those hot eternal seconds they have to decide whether to escalate the argument . . . or walk away and let the memory snakebite them another time.

Rosina crosses her arms, a known warning shot for the impatient Islander. She can sense her friends are having a problem.

— Is that us?

A second warning shot. 'Is that us' is Rosina code for 'I am happy to assist you in violently escalating this dispute'. The girls reluctantly edge away from the market stalls knowing Rosina's involvement would truly spell disaster. They know sticking around isn't worth it; the police would eventually get called and only Ginger Uncle would believe them. They walk away.

But perhaps in a bid to punish herself for giving in, Te Hoia turns back. She wishes she never saw the woman's satisfied face. She'll think of it for years to come every single time she is on this corner, a relishing grin felt for miles. When she's older, writing an essay of her own with Piopi in the footnotes, she'll describe the woman's expression as 'the cat that ate the endangered bird and got the clotted cream'.

Four

COCONUT JOKER

OUT IN THE WORLD, all three girls are now anxious. Just before they enter the gallery, Rosina spots an old Rolls Royce out of the corner of her eye, parked outside the shops a few stores up. She has a rare moment of silence as something unexpectedly seizes her.

Rosina had suggested the artists all have their exhibition here because this was the block where her grandfather used to sell school uniforms. He ran the School Uniform Exchange and Sponsorship Programme. The programme gave kids fresh from the islands uniform and school supplies if they couldn't afford it.

Rosina's grandfather was loved and neighbourhood-known before he died. In his final years, though, he was treated like one of the faceless swamp people who delayed 'the revitalisation'.

The uniform shop site was leased to wealthy kids with 'strategic moustaches and a coffee machine', as Rosina put it — made more painful by the fact she can never resist their coffee.

She becomes radioactive angry when she sees those familiar realtors in the street. Hawking like back when they'd shuffle outside her grandpa's shop. Always on their phone, looking for a swift and painless way to delete him.

Q can already sense what Rosina's about to do.

Te Hoia however is obliviously churning about the mouse-apron lady.

— That look on her face!
With your 'meat is murder' ass.
I was trying to help some nurses fundraise, shithead!

Rosina looks around and for one destined moment they seem to be the only ones on the street. Traffic has vanished.

— And like our people industrialised meat production!
No no no, that was your mob honey!

Q humours Te Hoia as she runs through all the imaginary comebacks they could have had.

They've reached the Rolls Royce. Rosina wraps her hand around the hood ornament. She relishes the moment with her taloned nails, suggestively. Q shakes her head, smirking. She would usually object; however, after the market incident she's in the mood. Te Hoia stops chattering and looks at them both, baffled. Surely not.

— No way.
No Rosina.
Plus I heard they manufacture them to hide inside the bonnet these days anyway.

— Yeah but this car is an old model.
She's gonna do it.

— What?
You never heard of CCTV?
Bro that's how they got my brother when he rode a wheelie bin like a bull, remember?

Pulling the steel bottle-opener out of her denim jacket, Rosina smiles. The bottle-opener just so happened to be her grandfather's.

— They don't have any cameras round these three shops, my Grandpa told me. He asked the council to install some but the council said no.

They weren't worth it back then.

BANG.

BANG.

— And well, now it's a rich neighbourhood . . . they'll presume they don't need cameras.

SNAP.

Rosina spins around in sweet disbelief. The 'Spirit of Ecstasy' mascot lies dented in her claws. All three girls burst into mind-blown laughter, although Te Hoia manages to stay disapproving through her howls.

— Oh you stereotype clown bitch!
Are you serious right now?

— You're right, it's the Irish in me!

— You don't know who owns that, it could be anybody!
You're gonna feel so guilty later.

They briefly marvel at the beheaded car hood, now pizzazz-free and sad. For those few minutes the girls are weirdly at peace. Rosina stirs on her feet and the others finally realise how under-cover drunk she is.

— No I won't.
My Grandpa always said
if you gotta choose between guilt and resentment, choose guilt . . .

A possessed look passes through Rosina's face like a cold front.

— Resentments eat away at you . . . make you go a bit funny.

They wisely evaporate and dart into the gallery, their wholesome facades glued tighter than ever.

Rosina stays privately adrenalised behind the face-paint. She kisses two of her older aunties who are beaming but also leaving. It's obvious why they feel uncomfortable. They tell Rosina they are so proud of her artworks — especially the one of her late mother. They are too earnest to mention Rosina's face-paint but one aunty tells Rosina not to throw the rubber gloves out from her artwork, they come in handy.

Te Hoia pushes herself around the space like a dumpling cart, still hissing and judgey. She starts giving weak smiles and limp waves to frenemies as she goes. She notes Rosina is the only brown artist in the show. She suspects Rosina is being jacked for cred but at least people are checking out the price list. Rosina has drawn all over their old school uniform jacket with faces from her family tree. Te Hoia wants so badly to buy it, or at least try it on. She also sees Rosina used a Union Jack in what is obviously a rushed sculpture about colonisation. As the grumpy friend, Te Hoia makes a note to grill her later.

Q stands dazed, finally remembering to eat the last of her controversial hot dog. Down the hatch. She slowly spots Rosina's signature big-face paintings from a mile away . . . not to mention a shit-ton of people. She bear-hugs Rosina.

— You really did this! Look at all this mahi!

And all these people . . . you're so clever!

The girls both squeeze tight, as if to juice one another. Q muffles into Rosina's mustard mop of hair.

— And I forgot to ask . . . why the hell are you in clown make-up?

Rosina touches her own face; the green and grey paint crackles like clay.

— Shit, that's right.

I just got so anxious about tonight, had to do something ridiculous to ease the tension.

— Well . . . between that and your petty crime, I'd say you're free to enjoy your night.

TOP LEFT 'RIP Ailini'
Acrylic on canvas
42.0 x 59.4cm
NFS

TOP RIGHT 'Gentrificolonic'
Mixed media installation
(flag, bottle, tube, gloves)
$300

ABOVE 'Q, Te Hoia and Me'
Acrylic on canvas
42.0 x 59.4cm
$200

The girls stay arm-entangled with watery eyes. Rosina exhales and laughs softly; she needs another drink. Her clown face failing, her grand-daughter stomach in knots.

— Is it a full moon tonight or something?
Why do I even still come here?
Be in these shows?

— Cos you gotta eat?

— This place man. It's a rotting body.

— That might be true.
But I'm still proud of you.
And it's 'our' rotting body.

They look around the white walls. Their neighbourhood is slipping away at lightning speed now and tonight, more than usual, they are scared. Rosina glimpses over Q's shoulder. She sees crabby Te Hoia already on the other side of the room wincing at works she obviously can't stand. Weirdly, Rosina only knows a quarter of the jam-packed room. She whispers into Q's ear.

— Who are these people?

Te Hoia comes full circle back to them, arms outstretched.

— Gifted artist by day, the Coconut Joker by night!
Um . . . why the hell is our portrait the cheapest thing here when it's obviously the best?
I'm not happy.

Rosina laughs so loud that some strangers look at her offended.

Q scowls back at them.

— Do these people even know it's your show?

— No. They just wanna be seen at the hip show about gentrification, so it looks like they weren't part of the gentrification.

A hand lands on Rosina's shoulder. It belongs to a handsome blonde boy. Q and Te Hoia side-eye one another. Rosina's white-boy weakness would be Shakespearian if it wasn't so predictable. They haven't seen this one before though. He gives Rosina a wry smile as he silently takes in her clown make-up. In response, Rosina rips the small woollen hat off his head.

— I told you I hate these hats.
Who you trying to be?
Wee Willie Winkie?

The two hold each other's stare . . . amused, blushing . . . to the point it's awkward for Te Hoia and Q to watch. After a few seconds and no introduction in sight, Te Hoia finally clears her throat.

— Um.
I'm just gonna go outside for a smoke.

Rosina nods, transfixed.

The fact that Te Hoia has never smoked a day in her life seems to have escaped her.

Te Hoia and Q trickle outside.

Five

HOW'S ANGIE?

Q AND TE HOIA step outside and start eyeing up the bus-stop already. Te Hoia knows damn well she's not going back into that damn gallery. They cross the road. Q pops into the petrol station because, unlike Te Hoia, she genuinely needs cigarettes.

— She hates gentrification till it comes knocking on her mick.

— Who even was he?

— And like . . . what is with today?
Bad juju or something.

The automatic glass doors part early for them. They step into the strobing lights, loud music and the back of a short queue. Te Hoia mindlessly grabs some gum while they wait. She spies someone she knows by the fridge. Standing by the relentless 2 for 1 energy drink special (that isn't even a bargain) is a girl Te Hoia used to be obsessed with, Angie. As is her embarrassed way, Te Hoia looks straight ahead until Angie has left.

She and Q arrive at the front of the line. The criminally overworked attendant who seems to have lived there since they were kids greets them with a smile. He's an old dude named Carl, Filipino; Te Hoia's mum knows him, apparently.

— Can I have a thirty gram of Settler Blues tobacco please?

— Do you want papers and filters?

— Yes please.

Carl opens the sliding door cabinet behind him and takes out a packet — a wordless, standard-issue khaki pouch like the rest. Te Hoia zones out and wonders where her old crush went. She peeks out onto the service station forecourt and in the distance can see Angie crouched down by the fence. She watches Angie clamber until her cloud of black curls and bell-bottoms are sitting firmly on the ground. Confused, Te Hoia moves closer to the chip aisle to spy on her.

She slowly realises Angie is sitting on cardboard surrounded by a few floral blankets. The hurt hits her as she recalls Angie previously living above the op-shop Te Hoia volunteered at. The shop is being made into a native plant terrarium shop with a matching native plant beer brewery. There was graffiti on the development for months that read something like 'REAL NATIVE PEOPLE < FAKE NATIVE BEER'.

Angie always had the coolest outfits and had a gorgeous little boy. Te Hoia remembers her incredible smile whenever she was browsing through the racks of clothes — her family were from up north too. Now she sits on flattened boxes and looks out onto the road, no little boy in sight. Te Hoia feels seasick with what might have happened to him. She longs to go out there but doesn't know what to say, or if Angie even remembers her. Q's unusually loud voice snaps her out of it.

— How much!? Since when?

— Yeah. Went up eight dollars yesterday.

— For a thirty gram?

Carl nods: he's dealt with these outbursts all day. A burly road-worker almost cried. He thought one under-slept teacher was going to punch him.

— Dammit! That's . . . nearly . . . that's like . . . half my rent!

Carl shrugs and grabs her a cheaper box to go. Q pays, then drifts away from the counter, stunned. She studies her runner-up packet of tailors. Te Hoia doesn't smoke, so gives few fucks.

— They put the price of smokes up!

— They always put the price of smokes up.

— Well . . . it's class warfare out here!

— No shit.
You say that every time.

— Cos it is class warfare every time!
Acting like they're selling brown weed or something.
You know what? I need a tobacco plant.
You need to get us some . . .

— Land to grow tobacco on?
Yep. You say that every time too.
They are literally called Settler Blues, I don't know what else to tell you.

They exit the doors, Q pissed as ever. Te Hoia looks over at Angie, hoping to catch her eye this time. Q is ready to go buy some weed and go home.

— Gonna go see my mate. You catching the bus?

— Yeah.
Hey, do you remember Angie?
That fly op-shop mum I used to talk about?

— Not really.

— I'm sure I talked about her all the time.

— Not to me.

Out of character, Q sounds weirdly competitive.

— Well then. What about her?

On cue, Angie turns around and looks Te Hoia in the eyes. Te Hoia involuntarily gives a gooey smile and raises her arm to wave. But recognition doesn't even mildly cross Angie's stare — she is vapour now. Her eyes return to the traffic. Knowing who Te Hoia is but not caring, Angie looks straight ahead until the girls have left.

Settler Blues
TOBACCO
RUM
WINE

Six

DEBT BEFORE DISHONOUR

AFTER STROLLING AND PLUGGING AWAY at her phone for a while, Q finally accepts her dealer isn't an ally tonight. The sun has been quick to dip lately and the light is vanishing.

Having carved up every corner by heart even with her head down, Q looks up to see an 'open home' sign. People are spilling out onto the street. Everyone is staring into pamphlets the size of colouring books, all identical to the large sign declaring this is a 'diamond in the rough'.

They all say that. Lazy copywriting.

You know they need me to be writing these sale signs.

I'd have these clowns bidding their asses off.

She joins the huddle and stares. Childhood landmarks up for sale are the new gory car accident, on this busy corner you sometimes get two for one. The house isn't a landmark by any means, just another comforting eyesore that Q had assumed was incapable of change.

She is convinced these people were invented only moments prior to this viewing, the same faceless actors hired to fatten out her most forgettable dreams and video games.

Fabrications at best,
butter-faced cattle.

Q's late aunty had a nemesis dating back to the fifties who played the long game. She came to the open home of her aunty's house after she had passed. The nemesis swanned around like she had skates on and lingered in the kitchen with a disarming smile (to the point people assumed she was the agent).

Clogging up
the back porch,
the council drains.
I wanna yell 'get off my lawn' but
I don't have one.

Evidently the woman dated Q's uncle for years until, out of the blue, he met and married Q's aunty. The woman never forgave her for the sweetheart theft. For that Q felt deeply sorry for her.

I did
until
I saw her relishing the deeds to the house,
pawing through my aunt's messy fiscal business.
Imagine your life laid out in hairy mortgagey detail
on your dresser
for all your romantic rivals to peruse.
I grew up thinking that, deep down,
money was just for show, no one really believes in it do they?
Some frozen greens that we push around each other's plates
with forks.
But girl I learnt that day
what the frostiest green tastes like!
It tastes like metal and wood that frames your aunty's face,
looking down on you,
screaming with her time-travelling eyes
for you to kick that bitch out.

Q's eyes fall to her phone.

She goes to jot the poem down, but her weed man has finally texted her back.

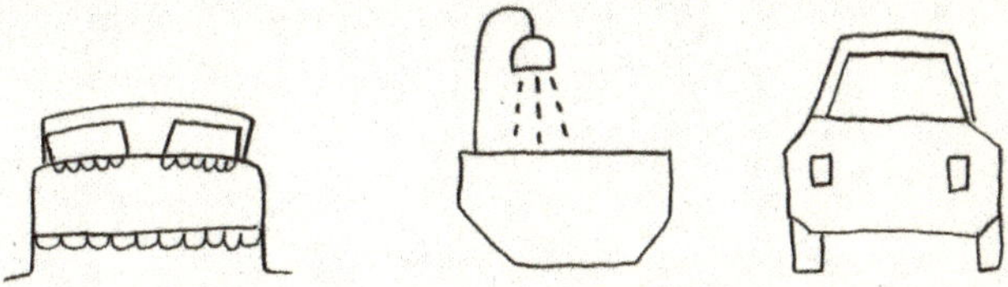

Seven

ARE YOU EAVESDROPPING GODS? IT'S ME, TE HOIA

TE HOIA IS BACK where she fears the Gods always intend her to be — uncomfortable on a bus ride home. Her heart is racing and she is trying to block out the noise. She starts to mutter to herself.

That's the third person I know without a house.

What the hell is going on?

Te Hoia's throat starts to feel blocked and her eyes get a bit watery.

They're pulling us out of our own soil . . . like weeds.

I'm not a weed.

She sees a flyer on the seat beside her. It's for an 'Islander-style party, bring a beer crate retro style, playing tropical jams'. Te Hoia doesn't know a single Islander who would promote a party like that in a million years, so she already knows the score.

I'm starting to hate this city.

Te Hoia closes her eyes and takes a deep, tropical breath. Angie's smile stains her mind. She looks at her book.

The book is *Mining for Mana: Pacific Property Development in the Twentieth Century*. Piopi Ruta-Chris published this back in 1995. The book's cover looks like a brown and cream tapa cloth but instead of a pretty frigate bird motif, there are tiny planes dropping bombs. It was an angry nod to nuclear testing in the Pacific which was still happening at the time.

Damn. That's Piopi for you.

Te Hoia turns to the chapter 'Psychic investments of those who wish to dismiss their role in homogenising the Pacific'.

OK, Gods, I know you can hear me.

Help me tune this shit out.

I gotta read these essays by tomorrow . . .

> We must be wary of every encroaching commentator who claims to assess and critique any form of Pacific Island migration fairly, even the smaller suburban migrations we are now forced to make. Particularly we must stay suspicious of those who dismiss gentrification and property development as unrelated to early colonial settlement. I am often forced to ask myself as a critic of such systems what I continue to uphold. Much is inescapable, we are all entangled. However I am talking about those dense, self-aware moments that we have agency and could choose not to comply.
>
> I often address and ask my fellow academics (no matter how earnest their gradient of privilege) to always appraise their personal intentions for the Pacific. I don't want you to hole up in the sanctity of your Western qualifications, either; I will still ask you what brought you here as a human being. Qualifications won't protect you from me asking you why you feel entitled to become an expert on my people. Academic merits are the new parking permit, and I say

this as a Doctor. What do they mean in a live turf war really? Who are we without them?

The detached journalists who have won Euro-prizes documenting our tattoos, our prisons and our homelessness. The academics accepting lucrative tenure to teach us back to ourselves. The cabinet minister given accolades for merely acknowledging the division that their imperial employer relies on. We must question every critical insight that frames us, especially from those not answerable to the frame. Within every level of our daily lives we must question those who examine us in any way but who, unlike us, may usurp and disband from their own findings whenever the sanctuary of good intentions is threatened or exposed.

You see, historical 'collaborations' on Pacific shores still have my cells begging for accountability. If you are as 'invested' as you say, then what 'returns' do you expect? Those who implicitly benefit from upholding the narrative of our oppression cannot continue to write themselves in as an agent of reprieve. If that is not what you intend, then what is it? Could you really handle it if your services were no longer required? What do you want?

Eight
TIME CAPSULE OF DISGUST

— What do you mean 'what's it about?'

— I mean . . . well, I know your mum died — you told me. I'm sorry about that.

THE CUTE PĀLAGI BOY is named Paul. He's seated and Rosina is at the sink. They've moved to the unused photo development room, just below the main gallery space — lights conveniently hard to find. In the murk, they hear sweeping upstairs. The permanently terrified gallery intern Latu is about to leave, but Rosina has the keys. This is temporarily her responsibility and kingdom to lock up. Water twinkles against her hands and the tin-can tub; she's finally wiping her face-paint off.

Despite not wanting to, Rosina sold the drawing of her mother and someone is coming back on payday to look at another one: so not a bad night. She feels clean and, apart from her hairline still looking like moss, she's right to think so.

A voice yells out.

— Bye Rosina! See ya tomorrow!

— See ya Latu! Thank you!

They hear a door slam and both she and Paul smirk to themselves in the dark.

— I just wanted to hear what it was about . . .
You know, from the horse's mouth.

— Well I'm not a horse and
did you not look around the
gallery?
Pick up a pamphlet?
Use your eyes?

She knows these white boys love it when she's mean to them.

She got through art school charging a much older man for the privilege.

— I saw the drawings. They were dope. I just wanna know . . .
more.

Rosina feels cute.

In a dark room being pressed to talk about her work by a handsome boy. A mediocre manic pixie dream come true.

— Well seeing as you can't use your own critical faculties,
I'm trying to pause time and commemorate the community
that made this area magical before they were blown to outskirt
smithereens.

Paul nods, trying not to seem in over his head.

— Y'know, like muscled out by the marketplace dominant.
People who buy land for sport.
Talk about us like ghost stories, but selectively remember us
when they're maintaining it's still cool to live here.

Paul looks blankly around the room, making out shapes. Rosina was impressed by her answer even if he wasn't. She sighs.

— Basically it's just a time capsule of disgust.
I'm just disgusted all the time.

— What was with that uniform
jacket?

Rosina feels a twinge. She presses on for the erotic promise. She's imagined Paul's pretty teeth against hers for too long to stop now. Knowing with that erotic promise comes the risk of attraction collapse, especially if they talk more.

— It's about the uniform shop my grandpa owned.
I told you that.
Four doors down from your studio.

— Oh yeah.
Did anyone actually go to that uniform shop?
I always thought it was a drug front.

Paul laughs but Rosina feels her hangover coming early. She dries her face with a piece of splattered fabric, insulted.

— You could donate old uniforms and help pay for students who needed assistance.
So no.
It wasn't a drug front.

— True, I never went there.
Sorry, white boy over here.

— Well your dad's got a knighthood.
You probably never had to oil up and fundraise dance for a school trip either.

Paul laughs again, a smug laugh that catches Rosina off-guard. His dad is a well-known actor who still does theatre locally and the odd bit of TV. He's been very supportive of his son's streetwear-inspired photography 'showcasing diverse models' he doesn't actually know in real life.

Rosina is realising she was too embarrassed to disclose Paul's work to Q and Te Hoia, hence the non-introduction. They'd drag her by the mop. She finds Paul's dad hotter than Paul, now

she thinks about it. At least he's seen some shit in his time. Her intuition starts to rise from its nap.
— 'Gentrificolonic' is a crack-up name for a work. Like colonic.

— Yup, good one.
You got it.

Rosina doesn't understand why she is getting snarky all of a sudden, except she does. Paul wasn't like this before. Wait, was he? She presses on, a horny optimist.

— Truth is, I wanted to get the hydrotherapy lady who just moved in next door to come in and do colonial colonics on white people who came to the show.
'Flush your evil ancestor out' kinda thing.
But Latu said health and safety was a nightmare.
And I realised I'd probably have to do one too cos y'know we all got dishonourable ancestors.
Duds in the blood.
But then Te Hoia called me a fuckin eugenicist!
And Q said I'm the last person who should be acting all pure about blood quantum.
They said I was showing my hazel-eyed ass!
It's a joke, but a bad one.
So I had to install that corny sculpture last minute.
That Union Jack, bleugh.

Suddenly Paul is kissing Rosina in the pitch black. His lips miss and push against her nose, warm on the bridge. He finds her lips eventually, to surprising effect.

They pause.

Rosina takes his warm prickly face into her hands, relieved. She can blindly feel his smile between her fingers as he starts to speak.

— But . . . like . . . isn't that racist?

Like . . . isn't that a bit harsh?

In that moment, Rosina is so grateful for the dark.

Paul can't see her eyes scanning the room for her phone.

(You can't fake an emergency and happily ride home alone without one.)

Nine

ARE YOU OK?

TE HOIA ENTERS THE OP-SHOP where she used to work. For some reason her university lecturer Whetu is behind the counter. In her fifties with a mop of black and grey curls, Whetu is wearing a pile of woollen blankets as a dress. This strikes Te Hoia as odd, as do the Christmas decorations for earrings. It feels like a comical escalation of Whetu's usual 'quirky academic' style, like she's unkindly cosplaying herself. Whetu gives Te Hoia a silent nod.

Te Hoia looks around the shop, a sloppy wobbly rendition of the store she remembers. It's still dusty and cramped. She can hear the familiar speaker hiss but for once can't recognise the music playing. It sounds like static is having a fist fight with a harp.

Te Hoia spies Angie in the corner. After the petrol station, this could be their chance to finally catch up. Angie is going through the clothes with her slender tattooed hands. She used to be a hilarious customer back in the day, fizzing and annoying other customers with her rowdy cute boy. Today her face seems covered in chunks of shadow. Te Hoia feels more determined to speak with her.

— Angie!
Did you get kicked out of your house?
You look like a sunken ship!

This is the moment Te Hoia suspects she's dreaming because she would never (ever) talk to someone like this. Sunken ship? Also, how rude? Angie doesn't respond to her.

— I wanted to ask you the other day how you've been . . .

Angie shrugs and keeps shopping.

— . . . and where your son was?
How's he?

— He died.

— How?

— Does it matter?
The outcome will always stay
the same.

— Are you OK?

Angie's eyes then seize Te Hoia with a clarity that nearly cuts through the dream. Angie's stare feels so real, fingernails-around-your-windpipe real.

— Ask anyone who has lost a kid if they're OK, Te Hoia.

The air locks.

— I guarantee you they'll take a lot longer to answer that question than everyone else you ask.

Angie snickers. She returns to ignoring and perusing.

Confused, Te Hoia turns to her professor for comfort. Her mentor Whetu tries to put it in simple terms.

— Look. It's like a plane crash. Some of us are like a black box:
we don't want to, but we know how to survive.
We dig deep and decide.
Every fucking day.
To bend, not snap.

Angie grabs her cardboard sign, blankets and bags. She pushes past them both.

— And some of us are like . . . the wing of the plane.
You know how people say 'she was never the same after that'?
What they're describing is someone who can scatter themselves across the ocean

— Pacific or Atlantic?

— All of them.
The point is, they don't give a shit if someone recovers them or not.
Lost at sea is better than the black box.
You know what I mean?

— Not really.
I've never been in a plane crash.

— I can tell.

Angie evaporates in the doorway.

Suddenly the op-shop turns into a pet store. The dogs are all wearing diamond necklaces and are barking silently from inside soundproof glass cabinets.

— Is this . . . Salties?

— Not anymore.
Did you finish the essay reading?

— No. Almost.

— Did you tell Q you like her?

— Hell no.

— Are you OK?

Te Hoia nods.

She now realises what a dumb question that is to ask someone who clearly isn't.

She lets out a loud cackle that rings throughout the store. To her surprise, she wakes up crying.

Ten

BOARDING GATE CLOSES SHORTLY

Q IS BACK in her room with music on.

She is writing poetry into an old exercise book. She reclines on her back, propped up with pillows and a fuzzy orange bird (Rosina and Te Hoia won it in the foyer of a diner from a claw machine).

Q puts the finishing touches on a poem called 'Brown Weed (I Swear When The World Isn't Scamming U It's Blaming U 4 Getting Scammed)'.

Your windscreen is a bubbly water,
some dude holds you hostage in the chrome pause.
He taps your shoulder while you stand at
  the crossing.
He raps to you within reason
Something along the lines of
'shilling out to villains why are we so willin?'
The cracks in the pavement mirror the cracks
  in his voice.
You hear what he's really saying:
Sis got a smoke?
Sucked mist and dregs,
the cost swells and I surf it up up up.
We are the mouthpieces of God,

which is why our lips are chapped.
A voice greets you when you knock off like clockwork:
Got a lighter?
Got a smoke to go with it?
Harmless
just a bit of blood in the sink
the odd solo huddle in the cold, I can take it.
They're acting like it's meth these days calm down:
Any of yous got a smoke?
And it'll go up up up
until:
how much did you say it was?
I started cos I saw a Playboy ad when I was 12,
who knew I'd be the girl in the turtleneck choking.
Another random red head with big titties
assuring younger me that 'no taste is smoother'
Sorry to bother you but do you happen to have a
spare cigarette thank you have a good day God bless . . .

Her older sister Sheena partially bursts in. Crispy glued-down lashes, curls tightly curated along her forehead and crown. Sheena's voice could melt a metal door. Q swears she can walk through walls.

— Q where is my eyebrow kit?

— Look at me. Does it look like
I've got it?

— Just because you look rats doesn't mean you haven't stolen my shit.

Q blinks. These kinds of entrances are nothing new, but they still take a moment to process.

Sheena moves her chubby French tips, forcing Q's door wide open. She has her hot pink blazer and black skirt on, obviously armoured up for work. Every night she looks amazing, and she is not playing.

— I'm on the graveyard shift Q.
Don't make me trash this room.

Q kicks back, knowing her soft unbothered voice irks Sheena more.

— Oh, I'm not gonna make you do anything.

Sheena works the airline counter for Pacific Jet. You know those beautiful dominatrix women who inform you you've missed check-in by nine seconds without a lick of sympathy or flexibility in their eyes? That's her. She has never once been rattled by an angry customer *or* fallen for their gut-wrenching pleas. Within her jurisdiction, she has won Best Ground Staff Manager three years in a row. Apart from scaring the principal at her son's school, it was the role Sheena was born to play.

— I'm sorry to interrupt your very deep poetry and I'm sure you're in a lot of pain.
But some of us have jobs.

Q doesn't bat an eyelid, not even looking up from her phone as she hits back.

— I gotta get up at 4am to go to my job at the bakery babe.
So I don't have time to steal your $8.99 eyebrow kit, which, PS, wouldn't show up on my brows anyway cos I'm not a wannabe Pālagi like you.

They glare mutually enraged for a few seconds.

— Not all of us make a song and dance about how hard we work.

Sheena raises her underserviced brows. Then they both burst out laughing.

— Well where is it then!?

— Are you friggin' deaf?
I said I don't know!

— I'm late.
Bye!

— Bye.

Q smiles as she hears Sheena's car zig-zagging out of the apartment block driveway. All bark and no bite since the day Q was born. Sheena's son is asleep and the coast is clear to spark up, chain-smoke and read her stuff aloud. Turning the page to a poem she wrote yesterday, Q takes a drag and begins to read. She mimes the words softly; they trail out of her mouth woven into the smoke.

Q sits on the windowsill and looks out into the other flats. She has work in six hours.

We Get It You're Of The Diaspora! A Poem (with subs)

The wounds of my household are held together only
by the blood that has dried between them.
Only I can curse out my sister
I will pop off if any of you even mildly make a dig.
I have no choice but to sit inside the mouth of
this machine.
It runs on fractured bone.
I gyrate on its tongue for seventeen dollars an hour.
When loudly telling your cousins back home to dream
bigger/grind harder,
try to consider they're working overtime just listening
to you.
Why does everyone recoil and hog me with such
pendulum lurch?
I buy 1B5 excercise books because I can't afford therapy.
No free healthcare in this jungle either.
There's British gelatin up my nostrils and down
my throat.
There's no brown therapists in this district anymore.
I checked.
Even if there was, I probably wouldn't trust them.
I gave a drunk woman directions to a bistro, it used
to be a church.
I didn't have the heart to tell her that before it was
a church, it was a feminine boy.

Eleven

BE OUT IN 10 MINS WAIT FOR ME BY THE PARK BENCH

TE HOIA SITS ON A BENCH about one block up from Q's bakery job down by the water. It's early afternoon and Q will be finished soon, but as per her shitty schedule, not quite. The harbour is small and peaceful for once; just a few hearty fishing dudes in their gumboots. The water's not as clean as it was in her teen days when she'd hang out down here pretending she liked boys, but otherwise it's like old times.

Kicking back, Te Hoia lets the sun do a quick slather on her city legs. She sits across from the local mosque. There are a few bunches of flowers along the fence line. One purple bunch in particular is rattling alone in the breeze.

No police remain but Te Hoia watches the meat zeppelin of a security guard drift along the fence line. Perhaps nervous, he gives Te Hoia a lipless smile a few times. It's funny how a chirpy sunny day only amplifies the morbid oddity of security staff and bereavement flowers. Te Hoia's mind starts to chatter as she waits forever on Q.

But it's not that odd is it . . . ?

All these events just linger and they make us sit in the mess and force us to awkwardly adjust.

It's all layers of wallpaper replastered and covered up over time.

The chatter stings and Te Hoia starts to annoy herself.

'Everyone gets used to it.'

But there's something in me that doesn't have that gene.

I don't wanna 'get on with it'.

I'm not gonna do that.

Te Hoia sits up straighter and takes in the domes of the mosque rooftops. She read somewhere they represent the vault of heaven. Looking up, she sends them all her will.

I promise I will never allow myself to get used to this . . .

I'll remember.

She feels an ancestor holding her accountable somewhere. They watch the purple flower heads play, head-banging along the steel bars. Te Hoia feels warmer for the company and at that moment notices the park bench she's sitting on has

[SOMETHING CROSSED OUT]
MUST END

casually carved into it. A nice tohu or a terrible omen — what's the difference now? Te Hoia gives the mosque security guard a smile of her own. She remembers a Piopi quote.

Even if the transience of our spirit is the only consistency we have, at least we can say we were consistent.

A loud honk blares out. Te Hoia looks up the street to see two drivers are hopping out of their fancy trucks to have a scrap. They're two big burly dudes in rugby jerseys, now standing and yelling at the traffic lights. Te Hoia squints and notices the men look like twins.

Two young boys come flying out of the bakery with white

paper bags full of food. Te Hoia wonders if this means that Q has almost finished her shift.

One of the boys yells something back into the shop. They must be no older than twelve these kids. They're far away but close enough for Te Hoia to know they're being punks.

Twelve

GERMINATING A SESTINA FOR NINA

AN OLD BIRD NAMED NINA goes to the bakery at the end of every day.

Q will give her a bunch of free stuff before she finishes her shift — without fail, Nina is always the last customer. Nina is almost ninety-three, an old school friend of Q's late grandmother. A tiny Pākehā woman, she knows how to play Q's exit like a piano. She talks her ear off with assorted cute stories and questions, which is why Q's shift always runs over by five to thirteen minutes. Tumble-drying and repeating her stories that Q will nod and respond to in fresh, respectful ways every time. It's never an issue; Nina is a welcome and sweet signal that Q is pretty much free. Rosina often laments the Pasifika condition of 'not knowing how to be jerks to old people, even when they're poisonous jerks to us,' but thankfully Nina is a non-event.

Every day Nina shuffles in, wearing a royal blue trench-coat with a matching blue shopping trolley and hair-rinse. She only ever asks for a lamington cake and a boiled egg but Q sends her home with a few loaves and (fried) fishes. Q is wiping down expansive stretches of metal bench before the owner's teenage son comes in and takes over.

— What did those boys just call you? I couldn't hear them.

— A fag.

— A what? My ears.

— An . . . idiot.

— Oh, that's horrible.
Why on earth would they say such a thing?

— I have no idea.
Do you want to take that last fruit salad home?
It won't be any good this afternoon.

Nina looks at the fruit salad and is genuinely taken aback. That's almost Q's favourite part of the offering; despite every day being the same, Nina is always genuinely shook by her generosity. Q puts the tub of fruit salad in a plastic bag and starts looking around for other things as she cleans.

— You know my grandson got engaged!
I wanted him to go out with you, but he lives too far away.

Q cackles.

— You're always trying to hook me up Nina!

— Well, you're a lovely girl!

Q throws in two pieces of coconut ice.

— That I am.

— She's a sweet girl though.
Her name is Emeni.

Q's ears flicker.

— Ooh, is she Tongan?

— Who?

— Your grandson's girlfriend.
It means Amen. That name. Is she Tongan?

As Nina processes the question, Q notices that she's wearing a little jacket with grey and blue squares. She looks like a patchwork quilt come to life and Q starts germinating a poem about Nina in her mind.

— I'm not sure what she is. I just thought she was Māori.

Q and Nina have these run-ins every so often.

— There's a difference between Māori and Tongan, Nina.
You might wanna clarify with her.

— Is there a big difference, do you think?

Q retracts a piece of coconut ice from Nina's haul as a private energy tax. She eats it as she tidies the drink fridge.

— Nina.
We've had this conversation.

— That's right.
I like you young ones, so stroppy.
They stopped saying Chinaman's Hill, too, you know.

— So they should.

— But the real estate lady still called it that.
I went to correct her and she looked pretty surprised.
I said, 'The young ones don't like that anymore Britta.'

Q flinches again.

— What real estate lady?

— Oh they're coming over all the time now.
They knock on my door and this one lady, Britta, she comes over once a month.

Q curses under her breath. The hum of the ovens, fans and freezers drowns her out.

— Fucking vultures.

— She says she's just being
friendly but I'm not daft.
Keeps telling me my section is
worth one and a half million.
I just tell her to get off it.

Q remembers the time she walked Nina home with her groceries. It was a tiny clapped-out unit on a humongous lawn.

— Well if she wants to play it like that, your section is actually worth over three million.
Next time she comes over tell her to fuck off.
From me.

Nina roars into laughter until she starts shaking and coughing. The boss's son Tan bursts through the PVC fly strips, fresh from school. Q notices for the first time that Tan wears the same uniform jacket that was at Rosina's exhibition. He gives Nina a knowing pat as he flies behind the counter. Tan chucks on his apron gearing up for the night shift and with genie-speed Q notices a fresh batch of chicken somehow already in the fryer. She and Tan are so at peace with the change-over they needn't speak.

— Alright. How are you getting home?

— Walking.
The doctor says you need lots of
Vitamin D at my age.

— I hear that.

Q grabs her bag and steers Nina out the door. She grabs a custard square and lasagne for Te Hoia and two cheese buns for the local icon outside, Larry. As they exit the fly screen entrance she waits for Larry's husky voice. She knows her next piece of choreography well.

— Got a lighter?

— Yes Larry.

— Got a smoke to go with it?

— Yup.

Q hands him her cigarette, her lighter and his daily bread.

Thirteen

THE BACK OF THE CUPBOARD

ROSINA SITS CROSS-LEGGED on a sloping footpath sprinkled with grass and pebbles. With a giant pad and some pens, she's trying to draw a house. The house is obscured by a development digger and some wooden boards. The homestead belonged to her great-grandparents and was the landing pad for four other families who migrated from the islands last century. Now her grandparents have both transitioned. The families that were housed there still chat on social media. The odd tacky but vital exchange, bobbing around each other like punctured life-rafts.

There was gossip about an apartment block going up in ten months' time; Rosina wanted to come see it for herself. The real estate signs claim the complex will 'house a whole community'. This is laughable considering these developers don't know how many people could squash inside her Nanny's house at peak capacity. Fifty times more likely these new occupants won't look like Rosina.

Rosina remembers Q comforting her as she sobbed into her beer one afternoon. Her Nanny was sick and Rosina was panicking about the house. All her cultural arteries to the city were dissolving in real time. She was ranting.

— Every time I look around another part of my life, of what makes me, 'me' is gone.

It's like that movie . . .
Attack . . .
Attack of the Body Snatchers!

She went to laugh but her voice cracked — then the whole facade collapsed.

Rosina covered her face in drunk shame.

Q grabbed her arm. Her voice settled sweetly on Rosina's shoulder as she rustled up another one of her accidental poems.

— Your grandparents live on in the giant pink letterboxes.
They're inside the roads.
In those big-ass rock walls that only we know how to make.
All their viral flowers these people don't know the name of?
All those scents and spores we invented?
They're our fingerprints.
They can't erase us, you really gotta stop saying that.

Rosina remembers peeking out from behind her wet sweater sleeves. Q was exhausted, slugging her beer. She then looked Rosina dead in the eye with advice straight from her bones.

— In these situations you either gotta get a grip, get a nerve or give in.
Those are your only options sis, so make up your mind.

Only the evicted can describe what it's like to sit across from a home you can never return to. And even then, they would never be so tragic or sentimental. Rosina's eyes shoot up and down, up and down. Pen scratching, the sound of smooth lines followed by darts and dots as she illustrates the guttering. She sketches the house and for a moment tries to include the digger, but in the end doesn't have the sportsmanship. Rosina eventually drops the pen onto the berm grass. She's glad she wasn't here when the developers ripped up all of her Nanny's banana-coloured roses

— that shit took decades to perfect. When Rosina stares at the house she can hear the sound of her Nanny's salu dragging along the concrete out the front. She can hear her voice too, explaining to Rosina's spoilt ass how a salu works.

The spine of the coconut is ripped out, a long thread, a husk.
And you grab a handful of them and tie it into a bunch and
it makes a broom.
And then you hurry up and clean up for your Nanny.

That wicked laugh. To think Rosina bought her grandmother a complicated vacuum-cleaner when she sold her first artwork. Her grandmother argued with it constantly. Once the neighbours came, expecting to break up a fight.

Rosina's heart slops around in her chest. She surrenders, letting the tears blip where they may. She vaguely remembers screaming at Q, drunk that day.

— Where do we go now though?
They're ripping up and rolling around in my Nanny's roses.
That's life, I know.
Doesn't mean it's fair.

It was at that point that Q wisely took the liberty of finishing Rosina's drink for her.

— No one wants to hurt our feelings so they keep exaggerating the city limits
'Oh but your Nanny will still be in the city!'
They just put our people in the back of the cupboard.
Like a bag of flour . . . full of weevils and shit!

Rosina started to sob.

— Everyone smells like my Nanny's roses except for me.
And they keep wondering aloud where my family went.
Do they ever bother to find out?

Follow that knot in their stomach?
No.
Cos deep down they don't want to find out.

Q just keeps rubbing Rosina's arm and watching her cry. Rosina inhales, pens scattered all around her in the present.

She wants to bend time and apologise for yelling at her friend drunk.

All she can smell on the wind now are the blooms they spoke of.

It's getting late in the day. Rosina imagines a world where people who get evicted from their homes get transported to a superior planet for free. There are hovercrafts made out of pearl. It sounds like something out of Q's trippy poetry. The vision slips away once Rosina hears someone chaining up the forklift across the road.

Rosina stands and awkwardly gathers her things. As she walks up the street, she puts her hand in her jacket pocket. The spice softly returns to Rosina's footing as she begins to twist the forgotten hood ornament around her fingers.

Her twisted laughter sets off a neighbourhood dog.

Fourteen

BLACK SHEEP WITH BENEFITS

Q HAS A STACK of new bed linen to drop off to her uncle. Flattened packets sit under her arm resembling classified files.

I look like I'm en route to represent someone in court.

This is notable considering this household has a habit of making Q defend herself.

She weaves through the back streets, sun and cicadas lighting her path. Finally Q walks down her uncle's gravel driveway and into the garage.

Her Uncle Taito scoffs upon seeing her. She feels the life-long familiarity of her shoulder blades tightening.

— What have you been doing all day?

Q could easily talk about the bakery, returning eleven library books, weeding the garden, getting her hurricane nephew to sit still during a haircut, or her plans to meet up with the girls. But Q knows to preserve her energy. She already knows her uncle takes a macho pride in not listening anyway. She gives him a hurled brick wrapped up in a smile.

— My days are busy but I won't bore you Uncle.

— Busy with sleep. You know your
cousin, he's still asleep in there.
Why are you all like that?

If Te Hoia was there, she would quip that late-stage capitalism in the colonies has all descendants of the working class depressed. Q opts for the fake cough brush-off, it's quicker.

Taito offers her a cigarette, which she silently accepts; it's the only thing they have in common anymore. Q sits down on an old folding chair. Taito makes his way around the parked cars and deep freezers, artfully moving rusty objects around for all Q knows. He tries to act like some ancient sage in his corrugated dojo. In truth he's only eleven years older than Q, a constant reminder that gatekeepers are often closer than they appear.

— Mum said to bring these sheets over.

— Where's your sister?
Haven't seen her.

— She's at home.

Everyone in the family loves Sheena. A cute kid, a job with family discounts, she's good at violent sports and she's a charismatic drunk. Sheena was also born into what Q calls 'invisible elderdom' meaning she was somehow always allowed to put people in their place ever since she was a child. It's probably why she bums people out for a living now and why defending Q is like breathing to her.

Any mediocre man off the street could swan into the carport right now and be given more authority than Sheena though. Uncle Taito is the kind of man who'd show a courier-bro at the wrong address more intimacy than his own wife. His face recently started to look a little blistered from alcohol but he would still be considered handsome by the aunties who play housie. Q twists in her canvas seat as he grumbles and paces around. For a few minutes he rearranges bags of ice in the deep freezer.

— You know the problem with all you kids?
Fiapoko. Trying too hard.

Ever since Q could remember, Taito had worked as a senior gardener for the council. She remembers wagging school in the park and having to hide behind a bin, terrified. Her uncle cleared away bush and scrubbed the local water fountain but she never got caught. Q decides to mess with him a little bit.

— I thought it was fiapoto.
Or is that something a try-hard would say?

Taito gives her a nasty smile.

— You think you're so smart eh.
But you kids blame everything on white people.
Cos you are too scared to look at yourselves!
What about all the knowledge you don't have?

Last year Taito had a fall and had to get accident compensation. He was told after he recovered that his seventeen-year-long job was now up in the air and that they'd 'be in touch'. Q tries to remind herself of her uncle's sacrifices so as to stay in grace. But lately Taito's taken an acidic disliking to her, even more than usual. He pushes the sides of his hair back. Q reckons in his mind he could still have a starring role in *Grease*.

— You'll never know what we went through.
But we never made excuses.
And we showed people respect.

Sometimes Q has to wonder if Taito even is her real uncle. She'd heard older cousins whisper that he wasn't. This reminds her of the cute time he said 'skull in the pantry' instead of skeleton in the closet. But Q knows not to let down her guard when he's like this.

— You act all clever but you don't know about that real shit.
Not like me.

Q wonders why she's always being accused of not working.

— Another reason.

— Another reason what?

— Another reason why your dad would be ashamed of you.

Officially over it, Q stands up from her seat. Cigarette still hanging from her mouth. She adjusts her jacket and sweeps her ramen waves to the side. Today has already been too long, yet she manages to muster a lemon-sucking smize. Q's unbothered mask remains her masterwork. In that moment no soul would suspect her heart of coursing with rage.

— Thanks for the smoke Uncle.

Q channels the rat she sometimes sees darting around there and struts out. Her boots hit the driveway and she can hear her uncle shouting out something behind her.

Though she is deeply conditioned to be a good girl and turn back, she doesn't. She knows now she may disengage whenever she damn pleases.

If I'm officially a disgrace, I might as well start enjoying the perks.

ICE

Fifteen
GANG BLUSTERS!

SHEENA OPENS THE DOOR, her hair is wet. She steps aside as Q dumps her bag down on the ground. The apartment smells like pre-shift instant coffee.

— Where have you been?

— Dropping some stuff off
for Mum.

Sheena can sense something is off. In her violent love language she intrusively holds her hand right up to Q's face.

— Look! Finally got coffin shape like you said.

Her nails look immaculate, an eye-watering hot pink. Q nods politely, all the proof Sheena needs that something's up.

— What died up your ass?

— Nothing.
Just seen Taito, that's all.

Sheena's eyes narrow, she balances her coffee cup between her new claws.

— And?

— And he told me Dad would be
ashamed of me for the millionth
time. It doesn't matter.
He's just going through his stuff
I guess.

— So?
I'm going through some stuff, do you see me talking to you like that?

— Well . . . I mean . . . yeah.

— Shut up!

The sisters cackle. Q already feels lighter.

— Ew. Don't worry about him.

Q slumps beside her nephew on the couch. He is hypnotised by his favourite cartoon *Gang Blusters* so he doesn't look up to say hello. Just the way Q likes it.

— I gotta get ready for work. Yous alright?

— Sweet.

Gang Blusters is a superhero team of friends who are also weather patterns. The subtext is climate change custodianship and occasionally giving a shit about indigenous people. Q thinks it's cute. Pretty strobey and chaotic, but it's relatable.

She can't help but identify with the Mist character, aloof and sensitive. Hilariously, Rosina looks like the character Heat Wave with her new haircut. Heat Wave also loses her temper a lot and fucks it up for the rest of the gang. But true to life, Q can't deny that the show would be crap without her.

Every time Q tries to chat during the show her nephew scowls at her (like his mother). Q smirks, knowing to let the discourse go until the credits roll. She eventually hops up to get them some juice.

At the sink she can hear a heated conversation coming from Sheena's room. Only half interested, she takes a few steps closer. Sheena's on the phone to someone, she sounds mad.

— That's all very well and good mate, but you can't speak to Q like that.

Q's mouth opens.

— She was doing you a favour. And she works all bloody day, what are you on about?

Finally! A work-ethic redemption arc! Q punches the air.

— Well! You got a problem you can come here and say it to me.

. . .

— Oh I'm not worried. But you should be worried about your secret girlfriend.

Oh you think I didn't know?

. . .

— Fat? Ha!

You and your ugly girlfriend bout to find out how heavy I can really be, mate.

Q clasps her hand to her mouth, trying not to scream.

— Oh please.

We're only six years apart, Taito, I can close that gap any time I like.

. . .

Anyway! Leave her alone. I gotta go to work.

And just like that Sheena turns on her hairdryer and starts singing along to a slow-jam.

Sixteen

RUSSIAN FUDGE-A-FUEGO

THE LOCAL TAVERN PARKING LOT converts itself into a flea-market on the weekends. Rosina is hungover, Q finally has the day off and Te Hoia is hungry for a serious feed. They congregate at the gate where a busker has stood unwavering for years on end. He has a cowboy hat and a full facial tāmoko, singing 'Let Me Entertain You' by Robbie Williams on his acoustic guitar.

It's the hot part of the morning, so as many people pile out of the markets as they pile in. Full bags and trolleys slam into the girls but they begrudgingly wade, knowing they will be the smug and snack-laden soon enough. Te Hoia sees her first victim. 'PANIPOPO' written on cardboard, the legendary coconut bun stand. She takes off into the crowd while Q and Rosina touch every item in the second-hand graveyard. Rosina holds up a baroque hand-mirror with a price she can't be bothered contesting or exploring.

— We don't really have a bartering culture here.
No one bargains or fights. Only a little bit.

— Yeah. We're more 'passive-
aggressive enquiry'.

— Oh boy, my mum loves a 'try-on and slow walk away'.

— The mind-games,
the loaded look.

— I'd say it was almost flirting, but this country tends to suck on that front too.

Rosina rests the mirror back on the owner's beach towel. She starts looking through a rack of leisure jackets. The old Indian couple selling them are wearing them as models/examples. They look fly as hell.

— Wait a minute, what happened to you and that boy?

— Who?

— The cute Pālagi boy.

Ol' Wee Willie Winkie.

Rosina snickers. She tries on a peach leisure jacket while the fly old couple silently look on.

— His dad's a knight and he doesn't know how racism works. Plus, he joked my Poppa's uniform shop was a drug front.

— Eh? What world did he grow up in?

— Exactly.

— I wondered why you didn't introduce us.

— Trust me I saved you the hassle.

Let's just say I was not aligned with my highest vibration.

— You gotta stop that fetish, man.

— I got white daddy issues. I know.

— To be fair your Daddy is a daddy.

— Can you not.

Te Hoia emerges from the crowd, somehow balancing a whole plate of coconut buns on one arm while feeding her face. Q and Rosina hook into the silver tray dipping the buns back into the cream. All three of them effortlessly chomp while browsing.

Te Hoia notices a pile of make-up and lipsticks in a basket. She combs through the inventory looking for any semblance of her colour.

— These foundations are all the same. Check out these names:
'Ceramic Glades'.
'Deep Pinewood'.
Oh shit!
'Russian Fudge-a-fuego'?
The fuck is that.

Q glimpses at the bottles to see if she qualifies only to remember she never does.

— And how they all say in smaller print NORMAL.

— NORMAL.

The only one who could get away with these pink Pālagi shades is Rosina, but she's in the distance trying on lingerie corsets over her t-shirt.

— She's never too hungover to plan her next drinking outfit.

Q does a light trawl of some kids' clothes for her nephew. Her fussy sister hates used goods, but Q makes a point to always get something for him. The selection baffles her.

— Blue grey green and ugly: dino print.
Blue grey green and ugly: truck print.
Lord if there's one thing I do not miss, it's my uncle dragging me round the boys' section.

— Speaking of the boys' section . . .

Te Hoia points. In the distance buying spring onions, it's a handsome sports journalist known for his women's magazine covers and septic homophobic diatribes. Q bursts out laughing as he tries to be 'down with his people'. Rosina, now on her third corset, spots him too. She squawks in the distance. The journo touches his fresh fade haircut before lifting a flimsy plastic bag from its hook. The girls watch him fill it up with potatoes, hexing him and his spuds. Q studies him conspiratorially.

— Should I go up and scare him.

— Offer him some panipopo like
Eve offered Adam the apple.

— Let's just say . . . he already knows me . . . and it wouldn't be the first time I'd have done that.

This stuns Te Hoia.

Her sockets are ready to bust if Q doesn't correct herself.

— Noooo.
Are you joking?

— We went to school together.
He was a friend of my brother's.
As the proverb goes.
I know too much.

Te Hoia screams while Q barely moves a facial muscle.

— Can you pass me one of those purses hanging up?

Te Hoia is still gasping but files through the used bags. She is slowly accepting that Q would never reciprocate her padlocked feelings. Q's past lives and private conquests could sink a government.

— Which colour?

— The Russian Fudge-a-fuego one.
Can you feed me a bun?
My hands are full.

Q opens her mouth and Te Hoia feeds her some of the coconut syrup and bun bread.

Q looks Te Hoia in the eyes. Te Hoia is taken aback but doesn't look away. For the first time there is an unexpected but decent crackle between them.

They don't actually fit her but Rosina bursts through the moment with two corsets she scored for five dollars. As per, she's steamed up.

— He got a nerve showing his face round here.
Look at his ugly face.

Q inspects him from afar.

— That's the annoying part. He's not ugly.
Rosina yells out,
— Yeah buy the potatoes to go with your fucking . . . homophobic . . . potato face!
Shouldn't you be at your made-up church!

The sports journo pretends not to hear her. Rosina watches him linger and head down another muddy aisle.

— I blame us.
We do it to ourselves.

Te Hoia can already tell that she disagrees.

— Excuse me, who do?
Speak for yourself.

— We're obsessed with making
our people into role models.
Then we give these role models
big heads.
Kiss their feet, treat em like
they're white Gods.
Then we act all hurt and shocked
when they turn around and treat
us like . . .

— White Gods?

Q rolls her eyes.

— Why you two always gotta talk so atheist edgy on a Sunday?
I thought I was the bitter ex-church girl in the group.

Te Hoia inspects Rosina's lacy items while throwing Q the tan purse.

— Man . . . wish I could fit a slutty corset too.

— Don't worry they give me a
middle boob but it legally fits.
Plus your tomboy ass would never
wear it.

— That's also true.
But maybe I would if I had a history of things fitting me.
Do you guys want some oka?

— Yes!

Rosina clocks the fish truck, all ice trays and white boots.

Q chooses a blue t-shirt with a robot on the front. She hands a beautiful blonde bogan with jet-black roots a one dollar coin.

— I want some panikeke too.

Te Hoia pipes up.

— Whatever you do, don't get a hot dog . . . remember, 'meat is murder'.

Q groans, the snakebite smarts as always.

The sun is slugging away and the bargains are flowing. Their bellies are a blank canvas. The sky and Sunday possibility still feels open-armed.

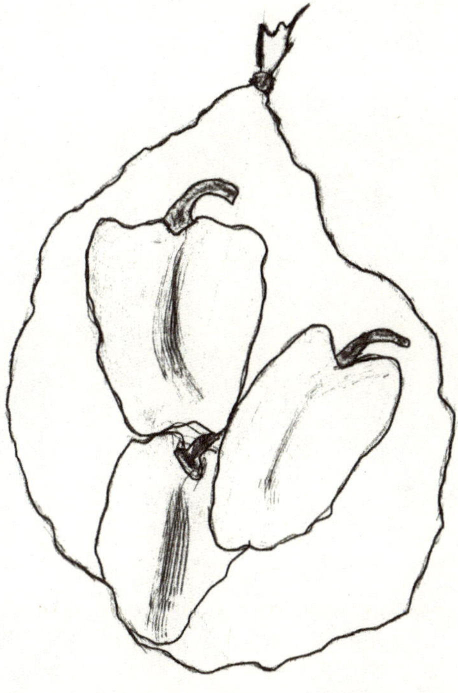

Seventeen

KAMRAN'S
CURRY
BURGERS
KEBABS
PIZZA
*FRIED
CHICKEN*

Q DROPS A CAKE OF COAL onto the foil tower. She holds the shisha pipe to her lips, watching the brick turn into whispers. The evening is cold but the strobing kebab shop and pop station keeps everyone cheerful.

She and Rosina blow the cartoon smoke onto the street in between jokes, the odd person walking through their drawls. It may be rose-scented but their exhaust is proving unpopular. One lady coughs dramatically as she walks through it.

Q remembers how one man yelled at her for blocking up the waterways with her cigarette butts here one night. *Fair enough* she thought . . . until he jumped into his spluttering diesel truck. She eyeballed him in his rear-view mirror, licked her trigger fingers suggestively and stubbed the smoke out with her wet digits. Quite the rebuttal.

Above them, big pūriri leaves drip over the awning. As Te Hoia slowly approaches from up the street, the waxy leaves start to slap together in the wind as if to greet her hello. Rosina and Q clap along until Te Hoia waves at the oncoming traffic like she's greeting a talk-show audience.

Kamran, the kebab king and Best Restaurant Street Food Winner (nine years ago) appears. He puts a plate of chips down with a side of hummus as per Rosina's request. Q continues her interludes with the shisha, as Rosina scoops up the chips. She shoves Te Hoia.

— How was studying?
Get your shit done?

— Yeah I did.
I read another Piopi Ruta-Chris essay.
I been thinking about it on my way over here.

— What was it about?

— 'Correlations of settler colonialism with modern examples of gentrification in the Pacific.'

— Wow. So a real party.

— Don't knock it,
she talks some shit man.

— I'd love to read it some time.

— I got it in my bag,
you can borrow it when I'm done.

— Why don't you just read it to us now?

— Eh?

— Yeah.
Why not?
We're cultured girls.

Rosina stands and curtsies with her mouth full of chips.

— I'm not getting napkins,
I'm getting 'serviettes'.

— You want me to read an essay to you?

While we eat and smoke out here
on the street?

Q pipes in.

— So what?
I want a reading!
You know I like your voice.

Te Hoia swallows her chip earlier than expected.

Faux-shy, she pulls her essays out. She chooses one that feels particularly poignant to the three of them, 'Strategic Losses in Translation: Exploitations of Manaakitanga and Coconut as Bootleg Blood'.

A woman with giant orange glasses appears, walking her dog. She tells Kamran to turn his music down, she can hear it from her house a street over. He's been blasting the music for seventeen years, so it's safe to assume she's new to the neighbourhood. Thankfully Kamran nods cheerfully. He eye-rolls and pumps the volume back up once she disappears from view. Q gives him a rose-coal smile.

The Kānaka Maoli of Hawaiʻi will hear tourists gleefully wire 'Aloha' into every festive nerve of the city. Many assume it only means hello, but perhaps 'the breath of life, love, affection, peace, compassion, farewell and the joyful sharing of life energy in the present moment' was too complex for the tourism industry to clarify — time is money, after all. And in the Pacific, pretending things are simpler than they are is a goldmine.

When I was younger, an uncle visiting from

Hawaiʻi told me that authorities could remove coconuts from palm trees in Oʻahu, so as to avoid a lawsuit should one fall on a tourist. I always wondered: How did this happen to this undercover portal of plentitude, our humble coconut? Why must it bear the brunt of our neuroses down below? How did something that can mimic blood plasma get reduced to such a bloodless transaction?

But this is how most colonial systems are upheld in the Pacific — strategic misunderstandings.

Māoridom in Aotearoa dictates that we gain prestige from manaakitanga. It is the connection and hospitality we express for those in our care but also to show all that they are our equal, they too have mana. What many may not know is that manaakitanga fortifies all those involved in its practice. The high-calibre nourishment that we express sustains our mana as much as those we give it to. Manaaki helps us unlock ourselves to the experience of service and activated respect. It is not pious or sacrificial in nature. It is not foolish either, however it has been mistaken for such and historically abused by settler colonialism. For Māori, manaakitanga is restorative of an unseen order, far beyond anything transactional.

The transaction, however, especially in the pursuit of dominance, is the calling-card of imperialism. The Crown, for example, must be at odds with manaakitanga in order to survive, because mutually embodying tikanga/ protocol would mean an instant relinquishment of the conquest and colonisation mindsets. Manaakitanga must strictly be exploited for gain; humoured at most.

On the 5th November 1881, troops marched upon the Western Taranaki settlement of Parihaka. Food had been placed outside the gates of this community. Singing children would greet the force.

This settlement (that would thereafter become internationally known as a revolutionary template of peaceful resistance) preserved and prioritised manaakitanga.

Even in the face of an invasion that would devastate their people, indigenous intention can remain more chilling for some historians than the spiritless invasions they endure.

In 'Cook' Island creation narratives, the universe was conceived inside the shell of a coconut. We see that—

— See, what do I always say?

They are snapped out of their wordy trance by an angry Rosina.

Te Hoia stops reading and takes the shisha snake from Q.

— We're too nice!
We get depicted as brutal round the clock,
when history *proves* we are literally too gentle!

Q catches a rogue pūriri leaf that was drifting towards their plastic white table.

Smoke gushes from Te Hoia's nostrils as she responds.
— My mum says 'manaakitanga says everything about you and it's how you leave this world'.
And it's kinda true.
It's not like Christianity, but we all know there's a karmic credit score.

— Are you sure about that?
Look around you.

Kamran comes outside for some fresh air and to enjoy his rowdy customers.

Kamran's kebab shop is a constant flow of taxi drivers, 'brothers' and family members. Things seem to have eased for a spell. Kamran is a handsome ageless dude, rings on every finger. He has a different polo tucked into jeans every day. He knows the girls by face but not by name. He couldn't possibly have the mental storage for every gang of brown girls who love him.

Owning this one-stop shop is his everything. A faded newspaper clipping of his young beaming face is taped to the kebab display cabinet when you enter the shop.

An extrovert to the bone, he often strikes up conversations when he's in a philosophical mood. He's heard snippets of their talk.
— Hey, can I ask you girls something?
The girls puff and nod.
— You know how here in New Zealand, the Māoris say Māui fished up the North Island?
The girls puff and nod.
— What kind of fish was it?
Q and Rosina laugh.

They lazily point at Te Hoia, their Māori representative for the evening.

— Some tribes say it's a flounder.
Some say it's a stingray.

— And what about the other islands?
The South one.
And the tiny one down the bottom.
Stewart Island?

Te Hoia takes a deep breath, warming up the lazy orator gene.
— The South Island is called Te Waipounamu.
Waters of greenstone.
I don't even know, cos they probably had heaps of greenstone or something?
But it's also called Te Waka-a-Māui.
They reckon it was the canoe Māui and his brothers stood on, when they were fishing up the North Island.
So they call the North Island Te Ika-a-Māui.
The fish of Māui.
I'm no expert though, don't quote me.
I'm a random Māori girl, not an ambassador for the people.

The traffic lights bounce off Kamran's face for a moment. He smiles and repeats it slowly back to Te Hoia, Te Ika-a-Māui.
— Stewart Island's real name is Te Punga-a-Māui I think.
The anchor of Māui.
They reckon it was the anchor Māui used when he was fishing all this shit up.

The girls laugh at her, but Te Hoia takes in Kamran's sweet face.

He seems genuinely moved.

— Do you think it's true?
Or is it just a story?

— True?
As in, do I think it happened?

— I don't know.
Maybe we are on the back of a big flounder!
It would be so crazy.

— I think . . .

Te Hoia has never considered this question before.

If she has, it's usually coming from someone not as sweet as Kamran.

— I think . . . it doesn't matter what I think.
Because I go with what it means to me.

— OK but . . .
what does it mean then?
To you?

— That I'm . . .
sewn into the sea somehow?
I genuinely feel that way sometimes.

Everyone breaks into a nod.

Te Hoia looks into the city skyline, chip in hand.

— So I trust that story.
And I trust that my people told it for a reason.
To me it's an anchor, it's a canoe, it's a fish.
Why wouldn't it be?

Rosina's Rarotongan side leaps out.

— And why wouldn't the world be born inside a coconut?

Kamran vibrates appreciatively and sips his espresso.

— I like this.

Imagination is kinda like . . .
a torch.
So we can remember what is true.

— In the cave of any faith.
Definitely.

Eighteen

PLEASE CHECK YOUR BALANCE

THE GIRLS STAND HUDDLED at the bus shelter, looking at each others' phones, blissfully scoffing at the online junkyard.

Q clocks a fellow tall, skinny Melanesian cuzzy, sitting beside them (but not before a keen-eyed Rosina does). With only one earphone in his ear, he squints to decipher the messy bus times scrolling along the sign. Once he has his journey sussed, he places the other earphone in and smooths his moustache for a few minutes. Q looks up from her phone and elbows Rosina.

— What are you gonna work on after this exhibition? What's next?

— Do some crying.
Yell at people to buy my work.

— Obviously. After that bit.

— I was dreaming the other day of doing a virtual reality project.

— Fancy.

— It's not like I have a clue how to do it. But if I could, I'd call it 'The World's First 3D Trauma Porn'.

— Uh OK . . .

— And you could charge rich people high admission prices.
It would be a tour of all the

homeless shelters, the prisons,
the gang houses.

— No offence but . . . sounds like something a white artist would do.

— Oh shit.
It does doesn't it?

— They'd win a prize. But you? You'd just get roasted, by people like me.

Te Hoia looks up from her screen.

— And me.
What were you thinking?

— The Pālagi genes jumped out for that one.
Yikes.

— Alright, alright, I get it.

A deep voice gatecrashes their critique.

— Sorry to jump in. Are you an artist?

The girls turn to the guy beside them. He's taken one earphone back out. Rosina perks up.

— Yep.
I am.

— I'm doing an augmented
reality diploma.
At the university.

— So you think I've got a good idea?
See!

— I . . . don't know . . . about that.

Q and Te Hoia burst out laughing. Rosina feigns shock, clutching her chest.

— But if you were looking for some help with VR . . .
I'd love to see your work . . .

I'm always looking for things to collab on.

Once again, Q and Te Hoia give each other half an eye each.

— Oh. Wow. Totally.

— Maybe you come by my new exhibition in town and we can have some tea.
Talk ideas.

He looks up and sees his bus at the lights.

He and Rosina swap details in a friendly blur, his name is Saulo — he's Papuan and Pālagi.

Once he's gone, Rosina begins her forensic examination on his profile while humming a wholesome showtune she just invented. Her breath quickens when she sees his cute face fist held high under a 'Free West Papua' page banner. Could this be her equally angry Pacific dream boy? Ready to free her away from the Wee Willie Winkies of this world? He runs a page called 'The Black Pacific'; it's quite enough for Rosina to initiate crush mode.

Te Hoia can't take the mature silence.

— He was cute.

— I know.
I'm not blind.

— Maybe you can make a standard 3D porn with him.

— Shut up!

The bus finally arrives, drowning their laughs out. Rosina seems to waft past the driver as she scans her card, scheming her future with Saulo already. 'Please check your balance' booms from the scanner with every passenger.

The driver is a Tongan woman named Trish, one of Te Hoia's favourite late-night chauffeurs. She has a light brown helmet of curls and a beautiful nifo koula smile, with gold on each side of her two front teeth. She is tall, even in her bus driving seat, and watches everyone in her bus mirror get organised.

The girls all flop down in the four-seater and continue to prod one another or adjust their reflections in the glass. After a few moments they realise that the bus still isn't moving. Q pokes her head down the aisle. She sees a tiny old man in a full tweed suit struggling to make his way onto the bus. He looks like one of her uncles. Trish pulls him onto the ramp supportively.

— Don't touch me please!

A croak that rings out on both floors of the bus.

The man pats down his pockets and seems to pull out white hankies each time. He begins to get irate and starts gasping, a bit confused. Q is on her feet. She has just enough to cover the man's fare. Before he registers what's happening she's already torn off a ticket and is returning to her seat. The man staggers closely behind, never actually thanking her. Trish gives her a nod of approval in the mirror, which suffices.

Q guesses correctly that, like her, the old man won't be venturing to the top deck of the bus. She is surprised when he sits with them in their four-seater, a curdling fit. The girls all smile politely and tap their phones. Te Hoia gets out her Piopi book; she's nearly finished.

— She was ugly.

The girls all look up at the man; a burnt nose and beautiful black eyes, he almost looks on the cusp of crying. Not the banter they were expecting.

— Sorry?

— Piopi Ruth whatever.
She was ugly.
Smart.

But into abortions.

— Oh. Right.

— Do you like that kind of thing?

— Um . . . abortions?

The girls wriggle, trying to fight off smiling. The man stares blankly. No one has any idea where this is going.

— No, I'm studying her.
But I do like her stuff. A lot.

The man doesn't seem to look away, so Te Hoia curtly continues.

— Us smart uglies have to stick together.

— I never see you brown people
on this bus.
Apart from the drivers.

Q and Rosina hold each other's stare trying to suppress their faces.

Te Hoia looks at him and can't ignore the irony.

— Dude. You're brown.

— No, my mum was from
Governors Bay.

Rosina stands. She adjusts her handbag and sweeps invisible crumbs off her front.

— OK bye. I'm sitting up the front.

Within seconds Rosina is up the aisle, seated neatly behind the driver.

Q nervously tugs at her long hair. She knows the girlies will punish her for paying this guy on. He continues to eyeball Te Hoia.

— You look fat.

Q sucks air in through her teeth and Te Hoia's eyebrows go airborne. She yells up the aisle to update Rosina.

— Wow, you're missing out back here!

Rosina could see it coming a mile off: her temper doesn't want to know.

— This just in — I'm fat!

Rosina waves her hand dismissively, fuming, looking out the window.

Te Hoia continues deadpan.

— Yeah sir, you can't say these things.

— And you . . .

Q pulls at her earlobe and looks out the window. She's trying to avoid any further contact.

The last of Te Hoia's diplomacy vanishes.

— Sir, you need to move seats and leave us alone now.

— I just wanna know one thing . . .

Q rolls her eyes. She covers her face so as to erase him from her eye-line.

Trish looks in the mirror while Rosina quickly pivots around. Te Hoia is very protective of Q, her whole body suddenly tingling. Q whispers while the man's voice keeps nagging away.

— Um . . . what's happening?

— Where are you people going?
Do you even live around here?

Rosina heard that part. She tilts her head like a Rottweiler.

— Ask yourself where *YOU'RE* going bro.
My friend only paid you on for three more stops.

— Fuck you bitch!

Rosina stands.

— You all good mate? Do you wanna go?

Rosina is already making her way down the aisle when the bus pulls over and stops.

Suddenly the carriage is a tight and silent balloon.

Trish stands from her seat and both doors open.

Te Hoia envies the black and white screen showing the blissfully unaware people upstairs. It's now a slow, dark night outside. Trish calmly announces that his time is up.

— We've taken you far enough.
Time to get off.

— But I . . .

— You didn't pay.
She did.
Get off.

— Ah fuck ya.
You look like a . . . tall cunt!

Trish just laughs and points at the outside world harder. It takes the man what feels like half an hour to disembark, but Trish is frozen the entire time. She stands with such badass assurance he eventually is left with no choice but to scuttle out like a crab. The doors clip shut and Trish turns her ignition key back to loud. The girls all wail, stomp and applaud. Trish lets out a relieved laugh, jaded head shaking along the roads.

Rosina prepares to get off the bus and includes Trish in her goodbye circuit of hugs.

She's a bag of hilarious retroactive threats after popping the buzzer.

— Why did you pay for him, Q!?

— I didn't know he was gonna be like that!

— Next time you wanna do that, give that bakery money to me!

The doors open and Rosina waves. She is pushed out to sea by a dozen top deck passengers. Te Hoia and Q watch her under the street-light, horizontally swimming out of view.

Q readies herself to get off too; Te Hoia lives the furthest away. Q reaches into her bag and calmly takes out a piece of paper. She hands it to Te Hoia.

— What's this?

Q's voice is strange.

— It's a poem.
I thought you'd like it.

— For me?

Te Hoia's face gets the hint and turns strangely hot.

Her body computes the gesture even if she doesn't yet.

— You always support my stupid writing . . . so I thought I'd write one for you.

The air and lighting dims between them.

Suddenly the old man has already been relegated to 'this one time'. Te Hoia studies the delicate stationary it was written on.

The bus pulls to the side, Te Hoia doesn't know what to say.

— I'll . . . I'll see you tomorrow?

— Yeah.
Come by the bakery.
Bye Trish!

— 'Alu a!

Q turns back to Te Hoia.

— I wrote it last night after my sister yelled at me for nothing. Let me know how you feel about it tomorrow.

Q's cheekbones raise into a sly smile. Turning away, too shy to say goodbye, she steps into the wind as the wheels roar away.

Bury Me a Pacific Jet Girl (For Te Hoia)

Bury me a siren of the salts,
retired hoe of the high sea.
Let my translucent nails point us both to
 the island we seek.
Bury me in the floors of the plane,
the one you steer while pestering Kong.
Surround his head like a buzzard with your
 barrage of brains.
Bury me amid the innervoices,
the leaks, the drivel, the cooked tirades.
Let me feed your mood fried food, it's like
 ghostwriting your stomach.
Bury me below the rotting picket lines,
hell no we won't go.
I have no fight in me but what I stashed for
 this flight with you.
Bury me a Pacific Jet Girl,
I will point at the clock and humiliate every
 Duke in your way,
make them lament their penchant for numerical
 time.
Bury me in the muscles of a flashback,
let our elders end on questioning octaves,
I don't mind.
Close the gates and still,
watch my volcanic rock roll through
like tall ice-cream
to your village.

Nineteen

THE ANSWER MY FRIEND

ROSINA WALKS AGAINST the whip-fresh evening, closing her eyes to it. Her place is only a few blocks from the bus-stop but she loves the walk. Amid the car-honks and dairy lights, her footsteps sound like Jack the Ripper crossed with a pageant piglet. She takes time to appreciate the freshly painted crossing that wasn't there this morning.

Everything feels different tonight.

I'm getting pre-Matariki feels.

Like I'm not even the same girl I was when I left the house today.

A slap of wind hits Rosina's face and blows her short hair around. She can hear the boulevard of deep fryers throttling. Up ahead a couple of teenage boys are hunched over a phone. Steam rises from their heads, dull with concentration.

Cool, the night is young . . . but not that young.

Maybe we have that in common.

Rosina had felt a shift between Te Hoia and Q these last few months and has been quietly sitting on it. They always assume she's not paying attention, but she sees all.

I only act boy-crazy and self-absorbed to take the edge off.

She lies.

It's cute or whatever but they better not forget about me!

She indulgently thinks of Saulo. Something cuts through her

delusions: could that be a genuinely promising feeling?

What if a year from now
I'm shacked up having an unplanned baby with Saulo
and I'll recall this weird but smug inkling I'm having now.
I'll say some shit like
'I knew the moment we met,' or
'When you know, you just know.'
And all that goofy shit.
I'll even lie and say,
'The thing was, I didn't have any expectations.'

Rosina can't keep a straight face. Undercover queen of the loathsome romantics.

Somebody's busted uncle hisses then makes a kissy noise as Rosina hits her final leg of shops. She screws her face up and speeds up the treadmill within. All women walk this speed when they're alone around here.

What's that thing they say . . . your cells regenerate every seven years?
Do we just . . . wake up one day like a snake and there's our old self?
A ghost skin . . . a husk, just awkwardly beside us?

Rosina imagines throwing her shell into the bubbling gutter below. It's just one of those nights when you quietly know you've changed for good, but you're not sure how yet.

She can smell chimney smoke; her house looks like the neighbourhood lamp. Cars are jammed up her driveway for some reason and she can hear music.

Rosina takes out her keys, the hood ornament is now a functional keyring gently tapping the door-glass as she lets herself in.

As she yanks it out of the lock, she notices for the first time the hood ornament is a woman with her arms outstretched, mid-flight.

Twenty

FINDING NGĀTI NGARO

TE HOIA NOTICES ICY DROPLETS on a few plants as she walks along. Summer always leaves the chat so abruptly.

It's rude.

One day I'm cutting my jeans into shorts, then I'm wearing a jacket that looks like a blanket.

Like literally the same night.

No grace period.

She looks around, still paranoid that the Gods can hear her complaining. Having lifted her head, she sees her bus-stop surrounded in those familiar orange cones.

Don't tell me there was a murder at the bus-stop?

I know they take a long time to arrive but damn.

Te Hoia really hopes they didn't hear that one.

There is a bright yellow card hedged behind the shelter glass and she notices that the bus timetable, usually a Las Vegas lit switchboard, is black.

Not another power cut?

She approaches the yellow sign, sipping on her water bottle.

THIS BUS-STOP WILL BE
TEMPORARILY CLOSED
OR RELOCATED UNTIL
FURTHER NOTICE

DUE TO DISRUPTION AND
CAPACITY ISSUES, THE 23, 001
AND OVERPASS EXPRESS ROUTES
WILL NO LONGER STOP HERE.
PLEASE NOTE THE 365 BUS HAS
BEEN DISCONTINUED

Te Hoia stands frozen. She feels like the overwhelmed nine-year-old girl she once was, using the bus-stop for the first time. There had been rumours about rerouting buses in the area but Te Hoia never looked it up. She'd seen the numbers dwindling, sure. Only now is she realising that she'd been virtually riding solo for months.

OUR BUS OPERATORS SUGGEST
THE ARTHUR ST TERMINAL OR
ALTERNATIVE ROUTES FOUND
IN THE MAP BELOW

Te Hoia glimpses the map and has an audible outburst.

— Ew! I aint walking over there, that's fucking twenty minutes away!

She looks around but the streets are empty. The lollipop man has long since gapped. The once shaggy road of pebbles now gleans like a supermarket cake.

Turns out the same pole she'd leaned on all her life was not the tōtara trunk she thought it was. Its roots weren't knotted to the Earth's core after all. Te Hoia's heart is thumping. She hears noise from a nearby garden and sees two birds hooning above the canopies screaming. She'd seen a nature documentary in high school that said birds do this when their chick has been stolen, eaten or has simply died in the nest. She remembers Angie's face.

She then hears a familiar twinkle and sees a text from Q.

Coming to the bakery?

Yep.
But guess what . . .
they wiped out my bus stop.
Like she's stranded?
Fight someone or cry?

Lol kalofae
but remember what I said to Rosina:
get a grip,
get a nerve
or give in.
I'll just wait here for you x

Te Hoia looks up from her phone and gasps for air.

Funny how a simple 'x' can regulate your nervous system. Considering Q's options of 1) resilience 2) retaliation or 3) relinquishment, Te Hoia doesn't know which to choose. She looks to the sun for inspiration, no longer flash-frying everything in its wake but still holding it down. She puts one foot in front of the other with no answer in sight. She remembers a mean nickname her brothers used to call her.

Ngāti Ngaro — lost fulla.

That shit used to make me so MAD!

As she bumbles past the last orange cone, it's tempting to think they may have had a point. She doesn't recognise her neighbourhood anymore, it's true. But there's one thing Te Hoia refuses to feel on her own land, and that's lost. She squashes up her button nose, lodging yet another promise to herself.

One day, I'll make all the people who tried to eject us wish we were lost.

I'm a lot of things.
But I'll never be that.
Te Hoia walks clumsily into the sun.

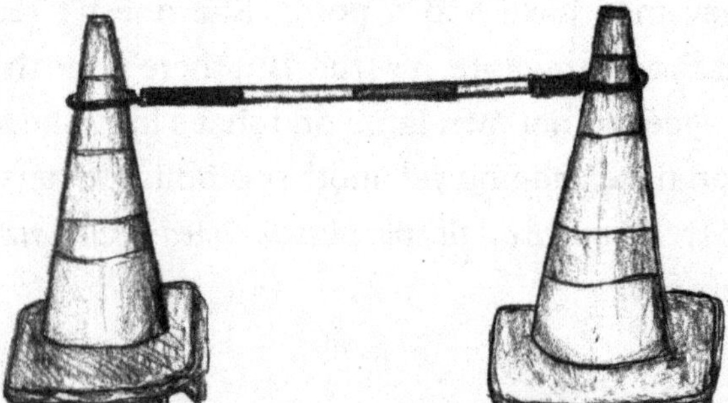

KUA MUTU/
END

ACKNOWLEDGEMENTS

Te toka tūmoana,
Ka tū, ka tū, ka tū.
Ahakoa i āwhātia mai te rangi
Whakapākākātia i te whitinga o te rā,
Te toka tūmoana,
Ka tū, ka tū, ka tū.
The rock stands in the sea,
Stands, stands, stands.
Although the weather may be stormy
And the rock may be roasted by the sun,
The rock stands in the sea,
Stands, stands, stands.

(Pepeha Taitokerau — Wiremu Wiremu)

Ko Ngātokimatawhaorua te waka, Ko Taniwha-Whakarongorua te maunga, Ko Utakura te awa, Ko Mokonuiārangi te marae, Ko Ngāpuhi te iwi, Ko Te Pōpoto te hapū. Ki te taha o tōku Pāpā, kei te hono au ki Hāmoa me Tiamani hoki.

I acknowledge all in my whānau, my chosen family, my creative and scholastic communities who have supported the creation of this weird but potent kaupapa. I thank all who have informed and infused my learnings upon releasing this pukapuka. To the Māori, Pasifika and migrant wāhine coming of age in Aotearoa, you have driven and inspired this work. Thank you for your tenacity, your mess, your hilarity and timeless energy. I should also thank all who have ever had the pleasure/pain to consider me a homegirl.

Between the lines, you are all in there somewhere.

Ngā mihi nui, thank you to my mother's Muriwai and Kingi whānau and my whanaunga from Utakura, Ōkaihau and Kaikohe. Fa'afetai tele lava, thank you to my father's fanau, with roots in Lefaga and Faatoia (Apia, Sāmoa), Germany, Liverpool and Tonga.

Thank you to the Penguin Random House whānau who have taught and guided me through this process. Thank you my amazing editors Claire Murdoch, Jeremy Sherlock and Faith Wilson for lifting this mahi since 2018. Thank you Louisa Kasza, designer Carla Sy and the whole Pingu team. Thank you to the Center of Pacific Studies at the University of Hawai'i, especially Tarcisius Tara Kabutaulaka. To all my Kānaka Maoli and Pacific mates there who schooled me, thank you. Bless the many inspirations for Piopi; especially Teresia Teaiwa, Haunani-Kay Trask and Moana Jackson.

Thank you to my first readers Akashi Zari Lee, Cameron Ah Loo-Matamua, Manuha'apai Vaeatangitau and Trish Tupou who helped me vet the early manuscript. Thank you to all the amazing artists, writers and musicians I collaborate with, especially my Kuini Qontrol, Studio Ki'i'pili, Aroha Bridge, Piki Films and Patreon family.

Ngā mihi nui to my parents, Dorma and Wayne. Thank you to my sisters Hayley, Kyla, Claire and Oriana. To my grandparents who to me will always live on Jessel Street. To my beautiful hoa rangatira Tokerau Brown. Every day you spoil and allow me to honour this mahi and by doing so, you help me to honour the memory of our daughter Te Hoia.

Lastly, thank you to the chaotic city of Tāmaki Makaurau from which I've burned, bloomed and rebirthed myself several times and on which I have vaguely based this book. Ngā mihi nui ki ngā iwi Ngāti Pāoa, Ngāi Tai, Te Wai-o-Hua, Ngāti Whātua-o-Ōrākei, Ngāti Te Ata me Te Kawerau ā Maki. Thank you to all communities here who, despite the eternal tussle with gentrification, colonisation, housing and death-rattle-stage capitalism, psychically endure and stay creating culture.

ABOUT THE AUTHOR

JESSICA HANSELL (NGĀPUHI/SĀMOA) is a writer, multimedia artist and musician from Auckland, long known by her rap nickname Coco Solid.

She is the creator of cult Māori cartoon *Aroha Bridge* with screenwriting credits ranging from the comedy *Wellington Paranormal* to indigenous soap *Ahikāroa* and is a long-time member of Taika Waititi's Piki Films, producers of her forthcoming science-fiction series *Jupiter Park.*

As Coco Solid, Parallel Dance Ensemble, Badd Energy and Fanau Spa, she has gained a loyal international music following and now heads artist-led record label and production house Kuini Qontrol, which also makes independent film, audio and animation projects. She is co-director of the Onehunga community space Wheke Fortress.

Hansell was named the Fulbright Creative New Zealand Pacific writer in residence in 2018, studying at the University of Hawai'i, where she started writing *How to Loiter in a Turf War* while researching gentrification in the Pacific.

The following year she was named an Arts Laureate by The Arts Foundation NZ.

Across all mediums, she consistently strives to prioritise Oceaniac narratives, wāhine, LGBTQIA expression and underground creatives of colour.